Still Dirty

Still Dirty

A NOVEL

VICKIE M. STRINGER

ATRIA BOOKS

New York   London   Toronto   Sydney

A Division of Simon & Schuster, Inc.
1230 Avenue of the Americas
New York, NY 10020

First Atria Books hardcover edition July 2008

ATRIA BOOKS and colophon are trademarks of Simon & Schuster, Inc.

For information about special discounts for bulk purchases,
please contact Simon & Schuster Special Sales at
1-800-456-6798 or business@simonandschuster.com.

Manufactured in the United States of America

1   3   5   7   9   10   8   6   4   2

Library of Congress Cataloging-in-Publication Data
Stringer, Vickie M.
Still dirty : a novel / Vickie Stringer. —1st Atria Books hardcover
ed.   p.   cm.
1. African American women—Fiction.   I. Title.
PS3569.T69586S75 2008
813'.54—dc22   200815346

ISBN-13: 978-1-4165-6358-7
ISBN-10:   1-4165-6358-X

This book, my fourth novel, is dedicated with my entire heartfelt thanks to three people who got me through the year 2007.

Mr. Sterling A. Williams, my Caleb

&

My celebrity couple, Mr. Rick Sales and Mrs. PriScilla Sales

&

*My biggest fan and sister, Frankie E. Stringer
This one's for you!*

Yesterday is gone forever, today is all that matters because tomorrow is not promised.

—S.B.

Still Dirty

Last time on Dirty Red . . .

*W*hen we last left Red, she and her boyfriend, Q, were running for their lives. Red had betrayed her former boyfriend, Bacon, by taking all his money and selling his house out from under him while he was in prison—and now Bacon wants his revenge.

In prison, Bacon wrote a tell-all book called *Bitch Nigga, Snitch Nigga* that gave the inside scoop on a scandalous setup and murder at a club that took down Q's uncles. Unbeknownst to Bacon, Red took the credit (and the money) for the book, which is causing quite a buzz on the streets: people are trying to figure out just who was actually behind the setup that took down the head of a major drug organization.

Red's friend Sasha had been ordered to kill Red by her imprisoned boyfriend, Catfish, but instead she hightailed it out of Detroit with Red's former love, Blue.

Terry, Red's girl since grade school, was obsessed with her man, Mekel. She went too far trying to get him back when she foolishly attempted to kidnap his baby. Unfortunately for her, her actions only caused Mekel and Kera, his baby mama, to become closer and Terry wound up in jail all alone.

We turn the pages to find Q and Red aboard a luxury charter jet headed to . . . Mexico . . .

CHAPTER 1

*B*acon arrived at the boarding gate just in time to see Q and Red's jet preparing for takeoff. Bacon's glaring eyes were transfixed on the walkway where his girlfriend and her latest lover had disappeared. Sweat droplets sprayed from his twisted face. He was furious that he'd missed his chance for revenge.

In a blur of motion, he spun around and dashed back to the counter, now focusing his deranged stare on the ticket agent. Speechless with rage, his wide nostrils flared and his breathing blasted out in ragged spurts.

For a moment, the woman was frozen in fright; her eyes gawked at the involuntary contraction of Bacon's jaw muscles. She gasped, hand clutched over her heart. She certainly didn't want her face to compare to the young lady's who just boarded the jet.

She looked as if she might break and run away, so he grabbed her by the neck and put his Glock to her dome. He held her face so close, her freckles almost jumped off her skin and onto his.

While he held the woman in his vise-like grip, thinking of Red's betrayal, Bacon's eyes glazed over with fury. It wasn't over. Red and her nigga could run, but they couldn't hide. Not from him. Bacon was gon' get his revenge—come hell or high water. He immediately flashed back to the letter that Red had written to him out of anger while he was in prison.

It would be virtually impossible for you to kick my ass, seeing as how you will be an old and gray bastard when you come home . . . I never loved you . . . I didn't even like you . . . I couldn't even stand the sight of your face . . . the sound of your voice. The words echoed repeatedly in Bacon's head. Although Red claimed she penned it out of anger, he knew she meant every single word. *You did all the work, but now my new man and I reap all the benefits. Wake up! You played yourself. Charge it to da game.*

Bacon's grip on the ticket agent tightened as a vein began to protrude and pulsate from his right temple to the center of his forehead. *Charge it to da game, huh?* he thought. *You'll see me again . . . face-to-face or six feet under.*

Bacon's thoughts returned to the present and he glared at the girl. "Bitch, where that plane going?"

"M-M-Mexico . . . Cozumel, Mexico."

Silence filled the air as the private charter jet finally leveled off in the clear skies. Out the plane window Red could see the blue horizon on one side of the plane and white clouds on the other.

Suddenly a claustrophobic wave overcame Red, causing her to heave deep breaths. She tried to calm her racing heart, which seemed to match the roar of the plane's engine. After observing her surroundings, she remembered that she and Q were the only passengers on the small plane. *He must have rented this plane,* she thought. *Damn, Q is living large.*

She held out her right hand, noticed its trembling, then hid it in her lap. She didn't want Q to see how frightened she was; after almost getting murdered twice in one day, Red was spooked.

What the fuck just happened? she thought. *None of this was supposed to happen. When did Bacon get out? Why in the hell am I the one runnin'? I control shit, not him.*

Absently, she cut her eyes at Q. He sat on the other side of the plane, two rows ahead of her. He continuously shook his head in disbelief. "I can't believe this shit!" he yelled out loud, clenching his fists on both sides of his forehead. He then took a deep breath and buried his head in his hands.

Look at him. I really fucked up now. I finally got a nigga that says he loves me and means it, but what about now? He could have gotten killed tonight because of me. Shit!

She turned her head to the right to look out of the window and felt a harsh pain radiate across the bridge of her nose. She began to raise her left arm to touch her nose, but a sharp pain stopped her. Bacon had damn near ripped her arm off when he grabbed her back at her house. Instead, she used her right hand and touched her nose. It felt twice as large under her fingers as she felt the damage. *My nose, my nose . . .* she thought, gingerly dabbing at the bridge.

Bacon immediately pushed the ticket agent away from him with unbound masculine force and sprinted back to the viewing station, only to see the plane on its ascent into the sky. He was so focused on revenge that he forgot that he had his gun still in his hand, fully exposed. He was startled when he heard someone yell, "He got a gun!"

With that announcement, people began to scatter like mice and pandemonium reigned.

"Run!"

"Duck!"

"It's a sniper!"

Bacon quickly tucked his Glock in the small of his back, and, trying not to draw any more attention to himself, beelined back toward the entrance. He didn't run, however, just walked at a more pronounced pace.

Bacon blended in as well as he could with the throngs of people stampeding out of the airport.

"That's him, that's him!" a female voice yelled.

Almost immediately, he felt a hand on his shoulder, and he instinctively put his hand on his piece. *If I'm goin down, I'm takin' one of these muthafuckas with me*, he thought. But when he looked over his shoulder, he saw that it was only one of the panic-stricken people in the airport, bum-rushing the front door trying to get out of harm's way. He let out a sigh of relief.

The next thing Bacon knew, two armed policemen bumped into him, but their eyes were looking straight ahead as they pushed him out of the way. He glanced back and saw that they were making their way inside, presumably to the ticket agent's counter. Somehow, she must have alerted them.

Bacon continued his trek toward the exit. Once he got outside, the light breeze swept over the beads of nervous sweat along his forehead.

He looked to the left, toward the executive valet parking, and noticed the BMW. His hurry to track down and kill Red and Q had been so intense, he hadn't cared that he'd parked the car illegally. Now there was a ticket on the windshield, an officer leaning against the car and a boot on the tire.

Fuck it, he said to himself. *It ain't my car.* It was Red's. Not wanting to stare too long, he stepped toward the curb, flagged down a cab and waited for it to pull up to him. Just as he reached for the door, he heard a voice cry out again, "That's him. That's him! I swear that's him!"

Bacon climbed into the cab in one smooth move and slammed the door shut.

"Where to, buddy?" the cabbie asked Bacon, looking over his shoulder as he merged into the exiting traffic.

Just as he pulled off, Bacon stared out of the window and saw the freckle-faced girl, with two officers looking around for her assailant. He ducked down until they got out of the International section of the airport.

"Where to, buddy?" This time the cabdriver spoke a little louder.

"Thirty-one-twenty-four Colonnade Drive in West Bloomfield." Bacon held his breath and prayed they didn't get stopped in a traffic jam leaving the airport.

As the taxi finally merged onto the I-94 highway, Bacon reflected on what that had just taken place.

Thinking about everything he had done for Red made his temperature rise again instantly. *I gave her everything. Bitch ain't never had to want for nothin', and now she wanna play a nigga . . . Have a nigga come to my crib looking for her?!*

"*You did all the work, but now my new man and I reap all the benefits.*"

Those words were permanently etched in his psyche. Bacon looked out of the window and noticed the scenery on the outside was moving just as fast as the images in his mind. *I'ma find that nigga and he'll be dealt with, but first things first.* Bacon grinned an evil grimace as he envisioned the perfect resting place for Red—floating under the Belle Isle Bridge.

$\mathcal{T}$he "No Seat Belt" sign came on and Red stood up to go to the bathroom. Her head pounded with every step she took toward the small, closet-like lavatory. She walked in, flicked the light on and closed the door behind her. The sight that she saw in the mirror made her dry heave. Her days of being a dime were over, she couldn't even get change. Red was fucked up. Not only did her hair give Don King a run for his money, her face told a different story. The swollen lump in the middle of Red's face confirmed that her nose was definitely broken, but to top it off, black marks were forming under her eyes, her top lip was swollen and her face was covered with scratches. *Bitch-ass nigga*, she said to herself as she stared at her reflection. *Where's a Vicodin when you need one?* she thought.

Looking down, Red also noticed bruises on her forearms. "What the fuck is this?" she questioned when she realized her shirt was wet. There was a faint stench in the air, but she hadn't thought anything of it. Now it was becoming more pungent. Red sniffed.

"Aw no the fuck he didn't!" She threw her hands up and hung her head. "This bastard pissed on my brand-new muthafuckin' shirt!"

Despite the pain, Red did her best, taking her shirt off and attempting to rinse it out in the sink, but the water pressure was low. She wrung it out as best as she could and put it back on.

Afterward she splashed water on her face and finger-combed her hair while she looked at herself in the mirror. "Get it together," she demanded. "You run this shit, not that muthafucka Bacon. I'll be back, you black-ass nigga . . . and the next time you see me, it's on . . . even if I die trying. Your ass is mine."

Red limped out of the bathroom and glanced at Q, who was looking out the window staring at the clouds. She wanted his attention but he didn't acknowledge her.

Look at Q. He won't even look at me.

Red trudged back to her seat and flopped down. She wanted to sit next to Q. She wanted him to hold her and tell her everything was going to be okay, but she knew that wouldn't be happening. She looked at him again and her heart ached. Red realized she'd truly fucked up this time and there was no easy way out.

What if Bacon had actually shot him? she thought. Tears welled in her eyes at the mere thought of Q being dead.

I can't keep on doing this shit. Q is a good man; all he wants from me is love and I can't even do that. Red thought back to her short-lived pregnancy and how attentive Q had been to her. *If I could only turn back the hands of time. Damn, Red, why you gotta fuck everything up?*

Red decided that since she couldn't change the past, she could at least make a vow to do better in the future. *Baby,* she said silently, as she looked at Q. *I promise I'm going to change. I can't keep doing this to you . . . to us. I love you and I'll be damned if I'm gonna lose you.*

As Q sat on the other side of the plane, he thought back on everything that had just happened. *None of this shit was supposed to happen. I shouldn't have stopped by that damn church when I saw Red's car parked outside. If I'd left well enough alone and just followed my plans, I would be on my way out of the damn country by myself to get away from shit like this. But, naw, my ass had to stop. Curiosity kills the cat.*

Look at her over there. He wiped his hands across his face. *That nigga almost killed me because of her. Time to cut my losses. Ain't no bitch worth all this drama.*

Q knew Red wasn't above a scheme or two—he chalked it up to games women play. But the realization he was going to become a father had taken Q to a different level. One that made him want to get legit and also allowed him to trust Red. Because of this, he'd wanted to marry her and raise their child together. Unfortunately, though, once Foxy revealed that the baby Red was carrying wasn't his, all of the love he had for her left his heart. Once again, he had been played by a schemin' ho.

Once we land, I'ma tell her it's over. I'm sure she knows, but just in case she doesn't, she needs to hear it.

Q thought back to the women he'd played to the left while he pursued Red. Although they still called and tried to get up on him, Q turned them down because he fell in love. He decided to mend those broken fences once he returned home.

Nothing like keeping my options open, he thought. *There's too many women out there that want to be with me and appreciate what I have to offer.* His mind wandered back to Red. *I'll speak to her on the streets, but that's 'bout it. It's over. I know she'll be okay. I'm sure she got another nigga waiting for her. Shit, she can even go back to that nigga Bacon. Ain't nothin' like two scandalous muthafuckas together. Yeah . . . he can have her dirty ass, but me and him, we have some unfinished business.*

As the cabdriver cruised down I-275 N, Bacon's thoughts were racing a mile a minute. Once they exited on 165, he noticed that the once-familiar surroundings of his hometown had changed. New homes and businesses reminded Bacon that he had been gone for way too long.

"If this shit has changed, I wonder what else has," he muttered under his breath. "Aye," he called out to the cabdriver. Dude kept driving. "Aye!" Bacon said louder.

"Yeah," the cabbie responded sharply, his cigarette dangling from the corner of his mouth.

"Take me to the Poindexter Village Apartments," Bacon commanded. He realized that going back to his house might not be a smart move. With all of the commotion at the airport, and technology growing every day, he suspected that someone could have taped something with a video camera or a cell phone. His heart raced with fear as he envisioned his face on the five o'clock news. There was no way he was going back to prison, especially over that bitch Red. Bacon noticed that the cabdriver peered at him through the rearview mirror like he was crazy. "You got a problem?" Bacon barked. "I said Poindexter!"

Reluctantly, the cabdriver honored his request.

"Suit yourself. It's your fare, buddy," he remarked, making an illegal U-turn, then heading back in the direction they came from. Bacon's heart raced quickly as he heard a faint siren in the background. The sound became louder by the second. The driver heard the siren and saw the flashing lights in his rearview mirror. He slowed and pulled over to the right.

"You stupid son of a bitch!" Bacon yelled at the driver. "You know you can't make no fuckin' U-turn!" He slouched down. When the siren was at its loudest decibels, he looked out of the left passenger window and saw an ambulance speed past. The driver pulled back onto the street and headed toward the high-way once again.

Bacon sighed in relief. He couldn't wait to get to Foxy's—the only place he felt safe.

Forty minutes later, the cab pulled up in front of a familiar place. Before he was locked up, the neighborhood was decent, but now it was outright pitiful. Screen doors were hanging off their hinges; some wouldn't close, and some couldn't close. Windows were boarded up and others were cracked. The kids that played outside were in desperate need of baths and working washing machines. Others needed combs to tame the wild, unkempt hair that graced their crowns. The kids didn't care how they looked. It was a beautiful early fall day and the weather was absolutely perfect. Not too hot, not too cold.

Foxy's place was the only decent apartment that didn't have anything hanging or cracked. He now knew why Foxy had a steel-gated door on her crib. He was sure that the other tenants didn't have the same taste she had when it came to decorating. She had an Ethan Allen theme going on that Bacon really liked. Foxy was always there for him and for that, he would be eternally grateful.

"Wait here," Bacon said gruffly as he unlocked the door.

"Uh-uh, buddy," the cabdriver said as he locked it back, using the electronic switch. "You owe me eighty-two twelve and I ain't movin till I get it."

Bacon looked at him like he was crazy. "Man, I ain't in the mood to be dealin' with yo' shit. I'ma get it; now, let me out the car." He pulled his Glock into plain view and taunted the driver with a screwed face.

The cabdriver's bladder weakened when he saw the piece; he

had no choice but to do it. He stared as Bacon ran up the steps, taking two at a time, and disappeared behind the door. Three minutes seemed like an eternity to the cabdriver, but when Bacon reappeared, he braced himself for what could possibly happen next.

"Here," Bacon said, nonchalantly, flipping a crisp $100 bill toward the cabbie. "Now get the fuck on." Bacon turned and loped back up the steps. He knew he would have to face questions once he appeared on the other side of the door.

"Q," Red whispered. He didn't respond. Red got up and shambled over to where Q was sitting. She gently placed her right hand on his shoulder. "Baby, I—"

"Stop, just stop," he interrupted and brushed off Red's hand. "I don't think it's a good idea for you to say shit to me right now, Red." Q stood up and attempted to walk away from her, but when he did, he brushed up against her and smelled her urine-soaked shirt.

Q scowled at Red in disgust. She saw the look of repulsion in his eyes. Suddenly, she saw herself through Q's eyes. She looked raggedy, and she even smelled her own body, so she knew she stank.

Red decided not to press him. She was already embarrassed enough so she figured she'd let Q come to her when he was ready to talk. She walked back over to her seat and sat down. Trying to get comfortable, she pulled her legs up to her chest, turned a little on her right side and clasped her arms around her knees—in the fetal position—and closed her eyes.

"So, that was that nigga Bacon." Q spoke in a low, deadly tone, after what seemed like hours, but actually only after a few minutes had passed.

"Yep, that's Bacon," she admitted.

"Were you going to say anything to me about him being home or was this the way I was supposed to find out?" he asked smartly.

"I didn't know he was home, Q," Red replied truthfully. She looked at him with an intense gaze. "Do you think I would actually put you in that type of situation on purpose?"

"What type of situation, Red?"

Red became silent.

"A situation where I could have gotten killed?"

Q had every right to be angry, but she wasn't about to admit to anything, either. That wasn't a part of her game plan.

"Q, all I did was go home. I didn't know he was in the house," she admitted. "Maybe he thought I was a burglar or something."

"Red, save it. That nigga know you ain't no burglar." Q began to raise his voice.

"But what I'm saying is, he hasn't seen me in a long time and—"

"How long is a long time?" Q yelled.

Red looked at Q like he was crazy. "Don't yell at me. I'm right here, I can hear you." She became silent again.

"Well, since you can hear me, whose baby did you lose, Red?"

Red craned her neck to the side. "What you mean whose baby? It was yours, you know that," she snapped.

"Do I?"

"Yeah!"

"What I do know is when you visited him y'all fucked. You lowered yourself"—he paused—"to fuck a nigga"—he continued slowly—"in the stall of a prison bathroom." Q looked at Red with eyes shooting daggers. "So let me ask again, whose baby did you lose Red, mine or his?"

"Fuck you, Q! Fuck you!" Red's eyes now welled up with tears. Her reaction told Q what he needed to know.

Q watched as Red's eyes could no longer hold the tears that formed. *Is that shit real or is she crying because I caught her in her own game? It ain't gonna work this time.*

"Save the tears and cut the bullshit, Red. I've known about the shit you've been up to for a long time, but I didn't want to believe it. I didn't want to believe someone so beautiful, someone who I would do anything for, would be so scandalous . . . so dirty."

Red now had tears cascading down her face.

"I've been with scandalous bitches before, Red, but baby, you take the cake. Even when you played my boy Zeke, he warned me about you, told me to leave you alone. Said you were poison, but I didn't listen . . . nah, I didn't listen." He shook his head as if he heard Zeke tell him to leave her alone.

"I knew you were using me in the beginning, but you know what, I was using you, too. I got what I wanted . . . some easy pussy, any and every way I wanted it. What you got from me was minor league, baby." Q spit his accusations at Red to inflict the most pain. "Then I started doing things for you because I was falling in love with you. Hell, I fell in love with you, but look what that did to a nigga. Almost got a nigga killed."

By this time Red was stone-faced and his anger was mild compared to the emotion she felt. Q just called her out on a lot of stuff that she didn't think he knew . . . stuff she would have never told him.

"Q, I—"

"When we get to Mexico," he interrupted, "I'm puttin' you on the next flight home."

Eyes widening, Red gave him a perplexed look.

"In case you don't understand what I'm saying, it's over." With that, he made his way to the front of the plane and sat down.

Red put her head on her knees and cried uncontrollably. *What have I done?*

CHAPTER 3

*F*oxy was Bacon's homie, lover and friend. Not only did she have the 411 on what was going on in the hood, her shit was always accurate. Everyone respected Ms. Foxy because when she caught her bid, she didn't snitch like a bitch. Doing her time like a man gave her mad respect in the streets.

Foxy stood about six feet and had the luscious curves of a woman. Her skin was soft and smooth. She kept herself up. Nobody would ever know of her past life. Although she didn't care if they did, she was comfortable being who she was.

Now she was in the kitchen wearing a pair of tight, skinny jeans and a cropped shirt that said "U want this" on the front. Her makeup was flawless and she wore her hair pinned up while she stood at the counter, dicing onions and green peppers. She sipped on some grape Kool-Aid through a straw just as Bacon busted through the door.

"What was that all about?" Foxy asked. "And why would a cab cost a hundred dollars? Where the fuck were you?" She shoveled the onions and green peppers into a pot of sauce on the stove and stirred the bubbly liquid.

"It's a long story," Bacon said, plopping down in a seat, "and I don't want to get into it right now." He took a deep breath in and let it out.

"Aw, naw . . . it ain't happenin' like that up in here," Foxy said with an attitude. She laid the spoon down, turned the pot down to simmer and sashayed toward Bacon. "Now, talk."

Bacon's eyes darkened with hatred as he began speaking through tight lips. "That bitch Red . . . I tried to kill her."

"Whatchu mean you tried to kill her?"

"I had her right here"—he motioned like he had her neck in his hands—"and I just shudda . . ." He looked at Foxy, who was now sitting next to him. "But then this pretty-ass nigga come to the door, ringing my bell and shit, looking for her ass."

"And?" Foxy questioned, trying not to show any emotion. She knew the pretty-ass nigga was Q.

"Shit . . . one thing led to another. Nigga kept questioning me about her ass, and . . ." He paused, and scratched his chest. When he did that, his shirt lifted up and Foxy saw the Glock tucked into his side.

"What did you do, Bacon?" Foxy's heart started beating as fast as a racehorse. "What did you do?"

"I did what any nigga would do. Handle shit like a nigga supposed to. I tried to blow both they muthafuckin' heads off." Bacon moistened his lips with his tongue, pulled the right side of his lip into his mouth and bit on it.

Foxy shook her head in disgust. "I can't believe you!"

"What the hell you talkin' 'bout?" Bacon snapped.

Foxy had heard enough. Now it was her turn to speak, but she chose her words carefully.

"Look, let me spit something at ya." Bacon looked at Foxy as she continued talking. "First of all, you gotta get a grip on yourself. How long you been locked up? You wanna go back? Huh?

"Secondly, I gotta give it to Red. Although I don't like that lil' stick-figure bitch, you gotta admit, she got her game tight. She got all of y'all catching cases for her, trickin' off money, putting her up in cribs and shit. Why you gon' get mad?"

"Why?" Bacon barked. "All the shit I did for her and—"

"Bacon, I understand that," Foxy interrupted, "but you're missing the point. You knew all along what that bitch was all about. You created a monster letting her have free rein over everything. It's over and done with. Move on." Foxy's voice was firm. "Why you gonna let Red jeopardize your freedom?" Bacon looked at her through squinted eyes. "Is she worth all the trouble?"

What's the hype with this bitch? Foxy questioned herself. *Niggas out here willing to risk death or go to prison over her. What the fuck?* She looked at Bacon quizzically, trying to will an answer out of his brain. *I know I can I can put my game down better than any bitch out here, and I'm a damn better woman than she is. But damn! Nobody can take care of you like I do . . . and you know it.*

Foxy started to catch feelings for Bacon when they fucked on the first night of his release while he was staying at her crib. She thought back to the last time they were together, and how he filled her mini-pussy with his dick. The memory made her shift her body position—uncross her legs, then cross them again—as she sat next to him. She was feeling horny, but she couldn't let that distract her.

"I know a lot more than you think," she said seriously, "but you have a lot to your advantage right now."

"What's that?" he questioned as he tightened his lips, turning up the edges. "I ain't got shit!"

"Your book, *Bitch Nigga, Snitch Nigga*, is the hottest thing since *Let That Be the Reason*, by that chick . . . what's her name?" Foxy tried to reach back into her memory bank as she snapped her fingers.

"Vickie Stringer," he clarified.

"Yeah, right, but anyway, don't let your desire to kill Red, or anyone else for that matter, land you behind bars again. Use that energy and explore a second book deal with Triple Crown Publications. Get back on top legit, then what happens . . ."

"Happens," Bacon finished her sentence.

He understood what Foxy was saying.

"Now, mister," she said as she slithered on top of him and placed his hands on her 36DD breasts. Bacon didn't have a problem fondling them. They felt just as real as titties on a real woman.

Foxy's voice suddenly took on a husky, sultry tone. "Why don't you gimme some of that big dick of yours? Ms. Foxy been missin' you."

Bacon smiled and stood up, the start of an erection bulging in his pants. Foxy wrapped her legs around him as he headed toward her bedroom. Deep down, he was glad she suggested it. Not only would it distract him from Red, but he'd been wanting to fuck Foxy since he walked through the door.

Bacon watched Foxy while he stroked her with his dick. Her breasts moved naturally with every stroke he gave. Bacon had to refrain from cumming because her virgin-like pussy gripped his dick like a glove. The money she'd spent on her sex change was well worth it. He couldn't hold back. Within minutes, Bacon came inside of Foxy, hard, and collapsed on top of her. He usually liked to start his sex game off with oral sex, but he couldn't mentally get to that point with Foxy. Fucking her was one thing. A hole is a hole, Bacon reasoned, but putting his face where she once had a dick didn't sit well with him.

Hours passed and Bacon stirred out of his sex-induced coma.

He looked at the clock; it read three-eighteen A.M. The few street-lights that weren't broken shone into the bedroom and cast a faint glow on Foxy's face. It was time for Bacon to make his move. He wouldn't be able to rest until he reclaimed what was rightfully his.

He threw on some clothes and quietly left the safety of Foxy's. Bacon roamed the streets, then caught an early morning bus out of Detroit, until he arrived at the home he'd longed for while in prison. Bacon noticed a police car cruise down the street with its lights on. He silently slipped inside without being seen.

The disturbance he caused the other night was not typical in his neighborhood. He was certain that Ms. Taylor, the neighborhood watchdog, had called the cops. But he felt confident that nobody had put two and two together because right before he dozed off at Foxy's he'd watched the news, and there was no story about a commotion at the airport.

Bacon tramped up the stairs, made his way into his bedroom and lay in his own bed. His mind began to drift into active thoughts while his head nodded, attempting to fight off sleep. He thought about Foxy's suggestion to contact Triple Crown for another book deal—a sequel to *Bitch Nigga, Snitch Nigga*.

They'll sign a nigga, he said to himself, but then he thought about the name on the book. Lisa Lennox. Bacon would have to find his way around the name. He then remembered that he burned the building down. That was okay; he'd find them again. Bacon smiled as he thought about the story. He would play out how he would get back at all who had done him wrong. He still had something for all involved. Q, Catfish and, most important, Red. As he closed his eyes and drifted off to sleep, he began to formulate in his mind his come-up and Red's demise.

CHAPTER 4

"Come on," Q barked at Red while he continued to take long, forceful steps around the Cozumel, Mexico, airport. "I need to find the closest ticket counter."

"Q, quit bullshittin'," Red pleaded and grabbed his arm to stop him. "You know you don't want me to leave."

"You think I'm bullshittin'? I told you I was putting you on the next flight back home and I meant it."

"Q, what about money? Everything happened so quickly. Do you have money?"

Q reached into his back pocket and pulled out his wallet. He only had a little over $2,000, and an immediate ticket like he wanted to purchase would take up most of his cash. He saw the check that Red had given him back at the church but he couldn't cash it in Mexico. Although legitimate, a check of that magnitude could raise a lot of unnecessary questions, especially being out of the country.

He reached for his cell phone. "I can call Zeke." Q decided to

Federal Express the check to Zeke in the morning and have him hold it until he got back. "I can call my moms. I got a list of folks I can call who can wire me some money," he spat angrily.

Red realized that at this point in her life she had nobody. She'd cut her closest friends, Kera, Terry and Sasha, loose; so she couldn't call them if her life depended on it.

"Q," Red said, changing her game plan, "it'll be impossible to get a flight out today."

Q scanned the flight monitors. "We're both emotional. Let's just find a place and sleep on it. We can talk about this tomorrow." When he found nothing on the monitors, he angrily stalked away while Red followed quietly beside him.

As they passed through the airport, Red's eyes grew as big as saucers when she realized how large the Cozumel International Airport really was. To her, it resembled an exclusive shopping mall. Everything a traveler could possibly want was within reach. She saw several overpriced stores selling everything from gourmet Mexican coffees to antiques to island attire. She even spotted a newspaper kiosk that had local and international newspapers, magazines, books and other items travelers might need.

Red's eyes bucked when she saw *Bitch Nigga, Snitch Nigga* in full view. Slowing down by the display, she busied herself looking through magazines while Q bought a newspaper, a pack of gum and a bottle of Advil. *Damn, it's all the way down here?* she questioned.

Red knew all about the buzz at home for the book but she had no idea that it was selling outside of the United States. She made a mental note to call Triple Crown when she arrived back in the states about her royalty check. *Looks like Lisa Lennox is gonna get paid*, she thought with a smirk on her face.

"What the hell you lookin' at?" Red snarled when she made eye contact with a customer who was checking her out. She knew she looked a mess, but held strongly on to Q in all her blood, funk and filth as if nothing was wrong.

Chatter of all kind filled the air and it seemed to get louder to Red, because of her headache.

A group of local children ran in front of them hustling for money by helping travelers gather their luggage and escorting them to the ferry.

Red sat down on a bench outside of the Hertz car rental counter and held her head, trying to get rid of the images of the attack that played over and over again in her mind.

"Oh, God!" she remembered calling out. *"B-B-B-Bacon . . ."*

"Who the fuck else?"

"Please . . . please don't hurt me."

"Bitch, you thought you would get away with your bullshit. Here we are again, just like old times. Did you miss me, bitch?"

Red remembered Bacon's hand going up in the air and after that, she couldn't remember a thing.

"Come on," Q called out, interrupting her thoughts. "Red, you hear me?"

She looked up through tired eyes and followed Q.

While they waited for their car to be pulled around, Q handed Red the courtesy tourist information he'd received. "Start looking through these for somewhere to stay," he ordered.

Red immediately became incensed. She thought he was trying to dump her off again. "Are you that fuckin' mad at me, Q, to where you would let me stay somewhere alone in a strange place?" She shoved the tourist information back into his hand.

"No, Red," Q snapped. "Remember, I was getting away. Away from you, from everything. I was traveling alone. I could have slept anywhere." He shoved the information back into her hands. "Ain't shit leavin' out tonight, so, if you don't want to sleep in the car or a motel, I suggest you look through this stuff and see what you can find."

Just then the porter drove up in a Chevy Malibu. She looked at Q and then back at the car and then back to Q again.

"We in a Chevy?" Red asked.

"Don't even go there," Q told her. He nodded toward the vehicle. Out of habit, he walked to the passenger's side door, opened it and allowed Red to get in. After she climbed into the car, he got in the driver's seat and drove off, merging off onto Boulevard International Airport heading toward downtown San Miguel de Cozumel.

Embarrassed and humiliated, Red rode in silence. She couldn't believe that she went there with Q. Her vulnerability was beginning to show. She knew deep down Q didn't want to treat her like he was, but under the circumstances, she couldn't blame him.

Red studied Q out of the corner of her eye as he drove, wanting to apologize for her outburst. His tight lips warned her not to say anything so she decided to just sit back and watch the scenery go by. In the distance, she could view the ocean, with its regal cerulean waters, so calm and serene.

Q stopped the car, but Red didn't look at him to see what he was doing. He turned the car off, got out and opened the door for her. They strolled along the Avenida Rafael Melgar, which provided a beautiful view of monuments and a striking view of the ocean. Along the street were many specialty shops that were inviting to anyone.

Green, exotic palm trees were scattered about along with Hawaiian ti plants, daylilies, bougainvilleas, date and banana trees. Everywhere Red looked off in the distance, the azure water sparkled like a turquoise gem. The leaves of magenta, saffron and indigo surrounding them were a far cry from gray and brown Detroit.

"Q, isn't this amazing?" Red asked as she stood in front of

him. She attempted to put her arms around him while she enjoyed the view.

"Uh-uh," Q protested, unclasping her arms from his waist.

"Uh-uh, what?"

"Don't touch me." He backed away. "You need some clothes and a shower."

"What?" Red challenged. She looked down at herself and saw that she still looked like shit, but still, Q didn't have to be so harsh. "Fuck you, Q."

"I was just sayin'. Look at you." Q turned his nose up in distaste.

Passersby began to watch the interchange between the two. "I ain't gotta deal with this! You need some clothes and a shower," Red repeated angrily. She stormed away, hobbling along the cobblestone away from him.

Q watched and shook his head while Red continued to walk. "Red, Red!" he called as he jogged toward her. "I wasn't trying to upset you."

"Whatever!"

Q reached out to grab her arm. Red flinched. It was the same arm that had the bruise on it. "What were you trying to do?" she asked roughly as she turned toward him. "You think I want to look like this? You think I planned this?!"

Q tried to suppress a smirk. *Women*, he thought. Red looked cute when she was upset.

"So now you think this shit is funny?" She raised her eyebrows, despite the pain it caused.

"All I was saying, Red, is I wanted to take you shopping. You tryin' to tell me your spoiled ass is turning down a chance to get some new clothes?" Q was anxious to get somewhere to buy Red an outfit. He was tired of smelling the old pee—tired of her disheveled appearance, in general.

"I don't give a damn. You got no right talkin' to me like that. You don't do it back home, and I'm damn sure you not about to start here, no matter *what* happened."

"Look, I ain't gonna argue with you about it. If you want some new clothes, I'll be right up there." Q pointed in the direction they were headed originally, then turned and walked away.

Red watched as Q ambled his way back up the strip and disappeared. A steady sea breeze blew and Red's stench caught her off guard. Feeling defeated, she followed Q. Although she was grateful to get some new clothes, she still planned on having an attitude with Q.

Once inside L'Chic Boutique, Red tried to hide her excitement while she perused the fine clothing. Picking out a multitude of outfits, she hung them over her arm. *He think he gon' get away with sayin' shit like that*, Red said to herself, *he got another thing comin'.*

After modeling several outfits, which consisted of Roberto Cavelli, Chanel and Michael Kors, Red didn't forget that her face was a mess. Before Q paid for her purchase, she grabbed a pair of oversize diamond-encrusted Gucci shades to complete her ensemble, but more so to cover her bruised eyes.

At the suggestion of customers, Q and the boutique owner, Red decided to wear one of her outfits out of the store. The owner pointed toward a restroom, where she was able to freshen up and change. The owner also gave Red a complimentary bottle of Island Gardenia body spray. Red knew what they were doing. She wasn't dumb, but, at the same time, she didn't complain.

They left the boutique, Red wearing a new outfit, and Q out of about $1,200. Feeling like a million dollars, Red stepped along the dirt-paved street, her sense of confidence restored. Although her nose throbbed against the bridge of her shades, somehow the fact that the shades were the coldest on the market and provided her anonymity made them well worth the pain.

Red noticed a group of young children outside of a flower shop. One of the kids, a gorgeous little girl with waist-length, wavy hair and golden sun-kissed skin whose color was complemented by the yellow sundress she wore, watched them closely. Within a blink of an eye, she ran toward Red and Q. The little girl presented Red with the most beautiful and delicate Star Robellini. Red had never seen anything like it.

Red bent down to the child's level and the little girl said, *"Para usted, mujer bonita." For you, beautiful lady.* She placed the flower in Red's hand and ran back to the shop. Red and Q looked at each other. She put the exotic flower to her nose and inhaled its beautiful fragrance. She had never smelled anything like it before; the aroma was indescribable. She held the flower for Q to smell.

He inhaled. "Umm . . ." he said. "It smells as beautiful as you are." The island's splendor was beginning to soften his anger toward her. Red removed the flower and stepped a little closer to him in hopes for a kiss, but Q marched away at the same strident pace he'd started at the airport.

Gotdamn, why did I say that? Q asked himself. *Shit!*

The farther he moved up the street, the more his stomach began to growl. They came up on a small café, La Perlita, and wandered inside. The smell of seafood wafted through the air. After they were promptly greeted, they were escorted to a small, out-of-the-way booth.

After their order was taken Red excused herself to wash her hands. Q looked out of the window at nothing in particular while thoughts ran rampant in his head:

I need to find a hospital. I can't let her walk around like this.

Fuck her, his lower self told him. *She got you in this mess. You're better off without her.*

I can't do that. He spoke to his conscience from his higher self.

Yes, you can. Get her out of your life now. She ain't been nothin' but trouble from day one.

Q turned and saw Red coming his way. *I do want her gone, but she looks so pitiful. I can't kick a dog while she's down.*

Sucker!

Red arrived at the table at the same time their meal did. Awkward silence filled the air as they ate. Nearing the end of the meal, Q finally broke it.

"Did you find a place yet?" Q knew this was a rhetorical question, knew full well she hadn't.

"Oh, shit, that slipped my mind!" With all that had been going on, Red forgot about finding a place. She grabbed the brochures out of the bag Q purchased for her back at the boutique and began searching. She asked for his cell phone so she could call various resorts and hotels. After being told there was no availability at such short notice, she finally lucked up on an exclusive resort property. Suddenly it dawned on her that because there were no other hotels available, Q would have to stay with her. *Good. Then I can work my mojo on him.*

Leaving a tip, the two left in search of their home away from home.

While they drove, Q saw a sign pointing them toward General Hospital and drove toward it. "What are we doing here?"

Q was silent. He knew she would protest if he told her. Reluctantly, Red followed Q as he headed toward the entrance of the emergency room.

"We need help here," Q said to a local girl who sat behind a counter. "My friend here, I think, has a broken nose."

Red cut her eyes at him. *Friend? I'll show him friend.*

"Here, sir," she responded in English, as she handed Q a clip-board. "Fill this out and have a seat. Someone will be with you in a minute."

Red grabbed the clipboard and sat down next to Q.

"Thanks, friend," she said smartly, glancing up from the clip-board.

Q brought the paperwork back to the counter girl once Red was finished.

"Raven Gomez," an unidentified voice called out within min-utes.

Red got up and followed a woman in a white coat behind swinging doors.

After forty minutes, Red emerged with her nose set in a splint, looking worse than it did when she arrived at the hos-pital.

Yeah, look at his ass now, Red mumbled to herself when she saw Q's reaction.

"Hey, baby," she said in a nasal-sounding voice.

"Hey," Q said, averting his eyes, unable to look at her. They left the hospital and headed toward the car. Red had an idea. She knew she always got to Q, and except for her face being messed up, she was looking good.

"Q," she said when they got to the car, "I was thinking." She grabbed his hands and put them on her waist. "When we get to the resort, we could . . . you know." Red pulled him closer to her while she grinded her pelvis into his. She attempted a smile and it hurt like a muthafucka.

Q looked at Red and quickly removed his hands from around her waist, not falling for her trap. "Get in the car."

She sat in silence as Q drove.

• • •

Q studied Red out of the corner of his eye. *She thought she was slick, trying to get up on me*, he thought. He smirked and tried to suppress a full-fledged grin.

Once they arrived at the Cozumel Palace, an all-inclusive resort, Q took care of the formalities, then located their living quarters.

"Q," Red said excitedly, arms lifted skyward as she sauntered into their room, which had a breathtaking view of the ocean. "This is beautiful!"

Q grunted and brushed past her. He went back out to the car and began to lug in their purchases he had made earlier.

Red looked confused when Q took some bags to one room, and some bags to the other. *I know she don't think we sleeping in the same room*, he said to himself as he noticed her watching him. *She got another think coming.*

Q brushed past her again to retrieve the last few bags. "Excuse me," he announced when he returned, trying to avoid bumping into her.

Red closed the door behind him. "Why are you putting bags in different rooms?" she questioned.

Q turned and looked at her. "You're kidding, right?"

Perplexed, Red looked at him.

"You really think you're sleeping in the same room as me?" Q shook his head in disgust.

Red's eyes scanned Q's body from head to toe when he swaggered into his room. Red knew his weakness and she was prepared to break down his defense mechanisms. *He's putting up a good front*, she thought. There was no way she was going to be on a beautiful island with a man as fine as Q and not get her way.

Q emerged from the bedroom and stopped in his tracks. Red had stripped down to the new set of black lace panties and bra he had purchased at L'Chic. "Gotdamn," he mumbled as he looked at her.

Don't give in, man! You're stronger than this, his conscience reminded him. He knew Red was up to her old tricks again, trying to entice him with pussy; no matter how hard she tried or how hard he became, he hoped that he wouldn't give in.

I knew I should have dropped her ass off at the LaQuinta close to the airport! Damn! Q was weak for Red's body and she knew it. Although her face was fucked up, her pussy wasn't.

Like a magnet, Q was drawn to Red and he slowly ambled over to her.

Don't do it, man! his conscience screamed. *Don't do it!*

Even though his conscience warned him, his manhood couldn't resist.

Red stood on her toes and placed a warm kiss on Q's lips. "Umm . . ." He allowed a small moan to escape his lips. Red's kisses traveled to his neck. Next, Q felt her hand inside his pants, grabbing his throbbing penis.

Gotdamnit, I told you!

"You want this, don't you?" he whispered, enjoying another one of Red's kisses. Feeling conflicted, for a moment, he didn't know if he was strong enough to fight off her feminine wiles.

"Let me show you how much," she said seductively and caressed the length of his manhood.

Just then, Q's hand met hers. "Uh-uh," he said seriously and removed her hand. Finally, the spell was broken. "This is off-limits."

Red's eyes bucked.

"See ya," Q strained to say cheerfully, then patted Red on top of her head and left.

CHAPTER 5

*H*ours later, the dawning sun cast a ray of light into Bacon's face. He stirred and blinked, relieved that he was no longer in prison. The last thing he remembered, he'd been in Foxy's bed fucking the shit out of her, but now he was somewhere else. A feeling of euphoria washed over him. Suddenly he realized he was finally in his home—the home that he busted his ass for, the home that Red disrespected, the home that he was taking back.

Even after the talk with Foxy last night, he knew he still couldn't allow Red to get away with everything she had done. He planned on getting revenge but knew it would just take time. Until then, he knew he had to get his shit together. *Nothing more dangerous than a legit nigga*, he said to himself. *They're the ones that get away with all the shit.*

He had planned to work for hours to remove any trace of Red's presence in the house. The first task was to remove the bloodstained carpet from the study, and the second would be to go through the boxes he peeped through earlier, but unfortunately, his stomach had its own agenda. The gumbo he'd eaten last night at Foxy's decided to make an impromptu visit.

Bacon dashed to the bathroom, peeling off his clothes, just as the cramps began to kick in stronger. He barely missed the toilet seat when he sat down, completely naked, as his rectum began to involuntarily expel the contents of last night's dinner. Sweat formed on his forehead. Since his bowels took longer to evacuate than he liked, he reached over and turned the shower on.

Maurice Clarence pulled up to the French Mediterranean–style home that he'd bought from Red and admired its elegance from outside. Maurice was blessed with the ability to ball like no other, which took him from the shady life of poverty to a life of unlimited income. At twenty-six years of age, Maurice had the life that most people wanted. His NBA contract alone was in the high seven figures, but that was nothing compared to the many endorsements he received. Maurice's popularity was not one without scandal. He was one of the NBA's most ghetto superstars: controversy surrounded him everywhere he went.

He walked as briskly as he could to the front door to avoid any unwanted attention. What he really wanted to do was get inside, sit down and ice his knee. Early in the preseason, a collision with an opponent had resulted in a torn ligament, forcing him to sit out the year. With him, his team had the opportunity to go to the finals; without him, well, the entire team was sidelined. At first Maurice was upset about his injury because he wanted to play. However, it was all good. No matter how long he was out, the money would still be coming in.

Putting the key into the lock, he turned to look at the neighboring homes. Maurice smiled. The peace and serenity of the area instantly soothed his mind. He turned back toward the front

door, turned the key and entered the home. Right away he noticed the boxes in the living room, and peeked inside.

"Hmm . . ." he mused, "I thought she would have had all of
her stuff moved by now." As he walked to the kitchen, he passed
the den. "What the—!" he exclaimed as his eyes focused on the
deep crimson blood that was now soaked into the carpet.

Alarmed, Maurice walked swiftly, opening doors to the various rooms, looking for anyone hiding in the house. He wasn't
afraid—he used to live in the Brewster projects, so he could handle his own if need be. He stopped in his tracks at a faint noise
and looked up toward the ceiling. Silently, he began to make his
way up the stairs to find out what was going on.

"Gotdamn!" Bacon grunted, feeling better after using the toilet.
Finally, he gathered his composure, kicked the bathroom door
shut and stepped into the shower to take care of his hygiene.

Bacon finished showering and turned off the water. The knob
squeaked as he turned it to the left to stop the flow of water. He
stepped out, dripping water on the thick thirsty carpet, grabbed
a towel from the linen closet and wrapped it around his torso.
He walked toward the mirror and wiped the steam away with his
hand. Turning to the side, he flexed a few times and admired his
physique until he heard something.

Creak . . .

He automatically reached for his gun, but he wasn't armed.
He looked at the stainless-steel towel rack and lifted it off the at-
tachment. *At least she ain't change this shit*, he said to himself
about Red. He stood behind the door waiting to swing.

Maurice looked down at the carpet as the floor beneath it
creaked. He continued to creep stealthily, but the sounds he

heard earlier had ceased. As he tiptoed upstairs, he saw clothes trailing down the hallway. He followed them and they stopped at a door to his right. In the air, he could smell soap. He put his hand on the doorknob and turned.

Bacon watched the doorknob turn, and the door began to open slightly. He saw something black jet out in front of him and swung the bar down hard, but a strong brown hand caught the bar in mid-strike. The men came face-to-face with each other and both glared.

"Who the fuck is you?" Bacon spoke, giving the intruder his most deadly sounding voice.

"I should be asking you that," Maurice replied with an even more menacing scowl. He kept his hand firmly on the bar as he sized up Bacon.

Just as Bacon attempted to jerk his arm back, the timbre of the intruder's threat—"Give me one good reason not to crush your cranium with this pipe"—resonated in his mind with familiarity. His eyebrows rose as he turned his face sideways.

Bacon looked up at the man, who was eight inches taller than him. "Reece?" he called out. "Reece, is that you?" A smile spread across both men's faces. "Nah, it can't be."

Isadore Jeffries and Maurice Clarence had grown up together in the Brewster projects. At thirteen and fourteen years old, the way of survival was hustling—there was no other way. Although Isadore was more street-savvy and cautious, Maurice tried to follow along just to be a part of the in crowd.

From the time they were young boys, there was something about Maurice that Isadore liked. Maybe it was his skillful way of handling the niggas when they played street ball, or maybe it was because he showed promise in getting out of the ghetto, but what he did know was that Maurice shouldn't have been hanging around him.

One night after Maurice and Isadore whooped up on some older cats in a fierce game of two-on-two, Isadore collected some major grip and started on the way home, but not before taunting their competition. As they walked home they ducked into an alley to divide up the money. Before they knew it, out of nowhere, the two older dudes they'd just defeated appeared.

"So you wanna talk shit," the taller one of the two said to Isadore.

"Man, y'all lost . . . fair and square. It ain't my fault y'all can't ball," Isadore continued to tease.

"You," the shorter one said to Maurice, angry that he'd embarrassed him. "Why you got all that blood on your shirt?"

When Maurice looked down, the short man pulled out a pistol.

Isadore knew what that meant, but Maurice was clueless. "Reece, run!" he yelled and dived in front of his friend when the gun fired. A painful sting ripped through Isadore's leg as he hit the ground but not before he retrieved his burner.

"Don't do it, man!" Maurice shouted.

"Give me one good reason," Isadore growled, then released a barrage of gunfire on the two men. The men went down instantly. Isadore looked to his right and saw Maurice running down the alley at record speed. Even way back then, Isadore knew that Maurice had a future and didn't want him to mess it up. That was why he had protected him, even if it meant taking a bullet himself.

Two days later, Isadore went to Maurice's house to learn that his parents had moved the family immediately after the incident.

Isadore was crushed because he didn't get a chance to say good-bye to his friend.

Bacon looked at the man who stood before him. He'd always felt like a big brother to him and was glad that he'd made it out of the projects alive.

"Go downstairs while I put my clothes on," Bacon suggested. "We'll talk when I come down."

While Bacon dressed, he wondered if Maurice was still in the NBA or if he had fallen victim to a dumb decision like Michael Vick. He knew he had the skills and definitely the height. Watching sports was a luxury in the joint. Many prisoners preferred football and boxing over basketball. They called basketball a bitch sport because there was no real contact.

"My nigga done came up somehow," Bacon said as he pulled up his socks. Although Maurice had grown several inches, matured in the face and obviously worked out, Bacon would know that voice anywhere. He'd never forget the timbre of it.

Within minutes, Bacon joined Maurice in the living room, purposely avoiding the den.

"So, how'd you find me?" Bacon questioned.

"Half naked upstairs," Maurice joked. They both laughed. "But seriously, I heard something so I went to check it out."

"I understand that, but why are you in my house?"

"*Your* house?" Maurice raised his left eyebrow. "I just bought this property."

"Bought? I never . . ." Bacon paused. Now he knew why all the boxes were packed. Red was not only moving, she'd sold his house right up from under him.

"You never what?" Maurice always felt that something was fishy about the sale at the closing.

"That bitch," Bacon muttered.

"What bitch?" Maurice questioned.

"That bitch up in my shit, got niggas all up in my crib, then she gon' sell it?"

"Oh, shit . . ."

"I shoulda blew her ass away when I had my chance!" Bacon picked up one of the boxes and hurled it across the living room. Purses spilled onto the floor, along with some of their contents.

"Calm down," Maurice suggested. He walked over to the mess and picked it up.

"I ain't calming down, man! This bitch took everything I had, then gon' lie about it. I left her fat and now I ain't got shit!"

Maurice looked through the junk and found numerous IDs, all in different names. "This the ho right here?" He held out a photo license.

"I swear I'ma—"

"Hey, hol' up, man. All this over a broad?"

"Not just a broad. She was wifey. She was supposed to be holdin' a nigga down while I was locked up."

"She fine and all, but that's exactly why I ain't settlin' down," Maurice admitted.

Both men dapped.

"Look, man, a bitch is a bitch, but a scandalous ho is like a rabid dog. It's fucked up what she did, but you need to get your shit together and calm the fuck down. I see you still hot-tempered." Maurice thought about something. "Hey, me and a couple of my teammates going on an all-male retreat in a couple of days. From the looks of it, you may need it more than we do."

"All-male retreat?" Bacon questioned as he looked at Maurice quizzically. "You on that DL shit?"

"Fuck you, nigga." Maurice laughed when he realized he could have used a better term. "Trust me, you'll love this re-treat . . . hos at your beck and call," Maurice confirmed with a sly grin. "So you down?"

Bacon nodded. "I'm down!"

CHAPTER 6

$\mathcal{F}$ollowing her botched kidnapping attempt of her boyfriend Mekel's baby, Terry was taken to police headquarters, 1300 Beaubien, where she was processed and booked. Afterward, she was strip-searched and given new jail attire. Not only was she humiliated by the way her body looked, she felt violated in the most inhumane way possible. The thought even crossed her mind that the female officer who searched her was a lesbian because she seemed to have been enjoying the job a little too much.

The walls of the jail were made of concrete and painted steel gray. You couldn't understand any conversations because the echoes of voices seemed to bounce back and forth off the walls. It didn't really matter all that much what the conversations were about, though; Terry was in jail for a foolish mistake and it all was beginning to settle into guilt and regret. Once placed inside the dorm-like cell, she found an empty bottom bunk to lay her thin mattress and blanket. Although the evening meal was served, Terry covered her head with the blanket and closed her eyes, holding back her tears of grief. It seemed like she had just gotten to sleep when her name was called for the morning court run.

Terry appeared before a judge at the 36th District Court for her arraignment. She was dressed in prison orange, with shackles on her wrists and ankles. She stood stoically before the judge while the charges against her were read—attempted kidnapping of an infant and aggravated assault. Those words tore through Terry like a knife and she cried uncontrollably.

"If convicted, you could serve up to ten years in prison," the judge said to Terry. "Have you secured counsel?" Terry didn't hear the rest of what she said through her tears and unintelligible mumbles.

"Miss Washington, I'm rescinding my decision to allow bail in your case."

Terry heard that. "Why?" she screamed.

"Your erratic behavior concerns me."

"Please don't lock me up . . . please!"

The judge carefully watched Terry before she delivered her final words. "I think you are a detriment to yourself and possibly others. Bail revoked." The judge called for another case.

Terry was whisked off to Wayne County Jail until her examination date.

Once in her cell, Terry knew she was utterly alone in her situation. She couldn't shake the memory of the way Red had glared at her and shook her head in disgust, then turned away, when she was handcuffed in back of the police car. *Red was my dog since grade school. She act like she ain't never did shit wrong. How she gonna just turn her back on me and act like I don't exist?*

Terry's anger was now getting the best of her. She thought Red would have at least come to the police station to explain to the officers that the situation wasn't as it seemed. *Whatever happened to staying down fo' yo' dog?*

What Terry failed to realize was that Red thought of her as

a charity case and everything she did for her was not without purpose.

Terry lay down on the hard bunk and tried to cover up with the one-inch thick, state-issued blanket.

"You wanna choose sides, then choose, but for your sake, I hope you choose the right one," she mumbled as she thought of Red's betrayal. Covering up the best she could, Terry went to sleep. Her heart filled with dread for what lay ahead over the next couple of days. Would someone come to see what was happening with her, or would she, in fact, be left for dead?

After Terry's initial meeting with her attorney, she had gotten a court order for a complete psychiatric evaluation. Terry underwent a series of tests and was assigned a therapist. Terry knew she wasn't crazy but if playing crazy would give her a reduced sentence, then so be it.

During the second counseling session, Terry began to realize that the sessions could be beneficial to her. It felt good to open up to someone who wasn't biased, who had the ability to help her work through issues that were clearly identified.

A timer rang, indicating that Terry's session was now over.

"Over so soon?" Terry said, somewhat exhausted.

"Yes," the therapist confirmed. "An hour can go by like that." She snapped her fingers. The therapist walked to her door and opened it, indicating to the guard that it was time for Terry to leave.

"Thank you," Terry said sincerely as she stood up and began shuffling toward the door.

The therapist smiled slightly and nodded. "Oh, and Terry, remember, it takes time. The first step is always the hardest but I know you can do it."

Terry nodded to acknowledge her statement, then turned and

began to follow the guard through the maze-like halls. Terry couldn't step to the beat of her heart because it was racing. She was anxious because it was time to meet with her counsel. She wanted to see what their plan was before she went before the judge at her examination hearing. She had only met with her briefly once she arrived, but Terry could tell she was well seasoned in the court of law. As Terry played follow-the-leader through the hallways, she reflected back on the two counseling sessions.

During the first day of counseling, the therapist sat quietly jotting notes, not saying a word, but allowing Terry to get everything off her chest. What the therapist noticed was that Terry never once mentioned Mekel's baby after it was born. She seemed stuck on the relationship as it was prior to then.

On the second day of counseling, things were different.

"Well, Terry, it seems like you've been down a rough road."

"Yes, I have," Terry said, wiping the tears away. She had just told her what happened the last time she was physically with Mekel and how he put her out of his house, naked. "If Mekel and I didn't argue around Christmas, he never would have gone to Vegas and we would still be together," she told her.

"I can understand why you feel that way," the therapist said. "However, let's focus on one person right now." Puzzled, Terry stared at her. "Let's focus on you." Terry blew her nose and held the wet and snotty tissue in her hand.

"But Mekel is the one who did this to me!" Terry protested, blaming Mekel for everything. "It's his fault."

The therapist walked from behind her desk and leaned against its front as she formulated her words carefully.

"Mekel did not make you responsible for his actions with Kera, so you can't make him responsible for your actions. Mekel did not force you to have sex with him, Terry. Mekel did not make you go to the hospital. Mekel did not place his son in your hands. Mekel did not do this to you, Terry." She paused for a minute and pointed her finger. "You did."

A chill ran through Terry's spine while she reflected. She recalled chasing Mekel around all the time. She couldn't hold a job because she was too bent on making sure Mekel wasn't fucking around with no other bitch. Her children began to lose respect for her because she neglected them for Mekel. She couldn't cart them around town while following up behind him, so she'd left them at her mother's more than she should have. Terry looked up at the therapist, her eyes filled with salty tears and her bottom lip quivering, and nodded in agreement.

"The first phase of the healing process, Terry, is identifying that you and only you are responsible for your own actions. Once you come to terms with that, then you can move on to the second phase."

"What's that?" Terry questioned in a scared, childlike voice.

"The second phase is to sincerely apologize to Mekel and Kera. It won't take away what happened, but it may ease some of the pain for all of you. Once that is done, then you move on to the third phase."

Terry looked at her with eager eyes.

"The third phase will come in due time and that is for you, Terry, to forgive yourself. This will be the hardest because you'll have to live with your decisions. No matter how hard we try, actions cannot be taken back."

Terry thought back to the therapist. She wanted to take her advice on beginning the healing process but was unsure if she could at this moment in time because she was still hurt.

After about a five-minute walk, the guard stopped at a steel gray door and opened it. Terry walked in and sat down. No more than thirty seconds passed before the door opened. A younger woman walked in, carrying a briefcase and two folders.

"Terry?" the woman asked.

"Yes. Who are you?"

"I'm Chass." The woman put her items on the table, then extended her hand. "Chass Reed. Your new attorney."

Terry raised her clasped wrists, indicating that she couldn't shake her hand.

After their initial meeting, the public defender, a middle-aged white woman, who was originally assigned to Terry, took on another case that was more high profile. Terry was now assigned the fresh-out-of-law-school Chass Reed. Terry had heard of people getting fucked by the system because the state replaces public defenders all the time. She took it for what it was worth and prayed that this change would benefit her and not make her just another judicial statistic.

Terry sat across from her new representative. Looking at the brighter side of things, she was glad to see that another woman was assigned to her. Not only was she a woman, she was a black woman. The apprehension she had a few minutes ago subsided and she felt comfortable, but despite Chass being a sista, she wasn't going to let her guard down.

Chass shuffled her papers, looking for something. Terry assumed it was important.

"Tell me what happened, Terry," the woman spoke softly, still searching through the papers. She stopped when she found what she was looking for. She looked at Terry over the rims of her out-of-date glasses, waiting for her response.

"Mekel used to be my boyfriend. We had a good relationship, or I thought we did."

Chass smiled and nodded her head for Terry to continue.

"I know this has nothing to do with it, but I loved him with everything I had." Terry stared behind the woman, at an invisible spot on the wall.

"I heard that Mekel was seeing other women, but when I asked him, he denied it and I believed him. Why? Probably because I wanted to. I never had luck with men. They all took from me and left me with kids they don't want to claim, but Mekel was different. He accepted my children and me. Because of that, I gave freely."

Terry closed her eyes and continued to talk. "When I learned that he got Kera pregnant, it felt like . . . like, I can't describe the pain, it hurt so bad."

She felt a tear cascade down her cheek. "Again, I didn't want to believe it, even though she confirmed it. I let my insecurities push him into her arms." Terry was shocked at her admission. She realized she was beginning the healing process.

"Terry, what about the baby? Did you intend to hurt him?"

"Chass," Terry said cautiously. "May I call you that?"

"Yes."

"Chass, I'm a mother. I've gone through some labor pains that would have you on your ass." They both laughed. "The baby." She paused. "I would never hurt a baby . . . mine, Mekel's, anyone's."

"What were you going to do with him if you didn't get caught?"

"Honestly, I don't know, but I do know one thing, I wouldn't have hurt him. That baby should have been a part of Mekel and me. If anything, I guess I just wanted to hold him," Terry admitted quietly.

Terry could tell by the way the woman's eyes glazed up and the quiver in her throat that she was moved by her story. Unbeknownst to Terry, Chass understood what she was going through. She'd stood by her man when he didn't have shit, and once he became something, another woman came along reaping all of the benefits that she should have had.

Chass slid some papers toward Terry. "I want you to look through these and tell me if these accounts are accurate."

Terry again raised her hands to alert her representative that she was unable to use them. Chass then moved her seat to the same side of the table as Terry and they looked over several reports. The first was the police report and the statements made by Kera and Mekel.

Terry shook her head and sighed after she read Kera's statement. Chass made note of the exaggerations that Terry pointed out in Kera's report.

The second report was information from Scott Memorial Hospital about the baby. Terry exhaled loudly in relief: the child had suffered no permanent damage from the fall, despite being dropped and suffering through a coma.

The third report looked foreign to Terry. "What's this?" she questioned.

"Blood work," Chass said, nonchalantly. She cleared her throat, then spoke. "Terry, I need to ask you a question; please be honest."

Terry wondered what else the lawyer could ask that she hadn't already revealed.

"How did you feel when you and Mekel broke up?"

"What?" Terry stared at her attorney like she was crazy.

"How did you feel when you and Mekel broke up?" Chass repeated slowly. She looked at a piece of paper with a lot of numbers on it.

"At first I was angry, then I got mad. When the baby came," she reflected, "I felt like I went into a depression and had lots of mood swings. I was sure if I didn't have kids of my own, I probably would have tried to kill myself." Terry knew for sure she was on the road to healing. It was now time to move to phase two.

Chass smiled. Terry validated what was displayed in her psychiatric evaluation. "Atypical depression." Terry saw that written on the paper with her test results, but she had no idea what it meant.

The thumping beats of Ludacris's "Money Maker" awakened Sasha. She blinked focusing her eyes on the scenery out of Blue's black convertible Cadillac Roadster. The early fall sun was bright in the sky, but the tint on the windows shielded her from the rays. The green leaves on the trees were at their deepest hue. Sasha sat up and rested her head against the custom-made headrest, enjoying the comfort of luxury. As they breezed down I-280 east, she looked to the left at Blue.

"Wha'sup, ma," he said as he smiled and bobbed his head to the beat.

So it wasn't a dream, she said to herself. *I really took Blue from Red.* She shifted in her seat. "How much farther?"

"Shid . . . about twenty minutes."

Sasha laughed to herself. *Niggas and they twenty minutes.*

Blue looked at her while she stretched and laughed. "What's so funny?"

"Red used to go to sleep all the time in the car." Blue reminisced on their weekend getaways. "Good ole Red . . ." He paused before he spoke again. "She was an eager student, always willing to learn."

Sasha noticed that he reached down to his crotch and adjusted himself. *I know this nigga ain't getting hard thinking about Red while I'm with him.* "Looks like she perfected her game."

Blue veered off onto the New Jersey Turnpike, I-95 North.

They were not too far from their destination. "You shocked me, though," he admitted, looking at Sasha quizzically. "You didn't strike me as a bitch who'd like pussy."

"Pussy?!" Sasha yelled angrily. "Aw, hell naw."

Blue ignored Sasha's protest. "Well, the way you ate her pussy, I almost came on myself. You see how I pounded that ass after you got it good and wet for me?" he bragged.

The memory quickly came into focus in her mind. *Get it wet for me, Sasha . . . Suck that pussy and get it right for me.* Sasha closed her eyes in shame as she remembered how Red held her head, forcing her into her pussy until she came. Sasha did what Blue asked her to do only for him to mount Red and fuck her.

"Fuck that bitch Red. And if I did fuck women, I definitely wouldn't fuck a dirty-ass bitch like her. Ho think she all that, but truth be told, she ain't shit." Sasha snapped. She didn't like Blue disrespecting her the way he did.

"Slow yo' roll, ma!" Blue warned. "Regardless what you say, you can only respect her game. It was *you* who had *your* face in *her* pussy. Not the other way around."

"Why you glorifying that dirty bitch? You just another nigga she played."

The car finally came to a stop in an exclusive residential neighborhood in New York. Sasha tried to look out of the window to take in her surroundings, but Blue turned toward Sasha and grabbed her chin with his thumb and forefinger. "Looks like you got a lot to say, but right now, yo' mouth gon' get you in a lotta trouble. Now, you called me. That means that I talk and you shut the fuck up. I ain't got no problem giving you anything you want, but I ain't got no problem with knocking you on yo' ass, either." Blue moved his face within inches of Sasha's. "It's your choice."

With that, he released Sasha and exited the car. Sasha fought back the tears that formed as she rubbed her chin. She knew what he said was right. She had no employable job skills and she knew this. The only thing she knew was being wifey; and with Red still in Blue's mind, she wondered if she would ever get that title.

Sasha was used to living off niggas and made a living doing so. *It's gonna be some shit when Red finds out I'm with this nigga,* she thought. *I should have got rid of her when I had a chance.* Her conscience spoke back to her. *That's not you, Sasha. Tell that nigga Catfish to do it himself.* Then she thought, *I need to do something, because when Catfish realizes I'm gone and Red is still alive, it's gonna be hell to pay.* Sasha knew she was doomed. She had nothing, and with nothing, she knew she was shit. She made her decision. She got out of the car and obediently followed Blue.

CHAPTER 7

*E*very day that passed increased the tension between Red and Q. During the first few days, he went sightseeing, shopping and to a local club alone. He came back late in the night to avoid Red. The rest of the week, he was gone before she woke up. He didn't want to be around her. Not only was he still mad at her, he just couldn't trust his little head to be rational.

Red was appreciative of the downtime because it gave her body a chance to heal but most of all, it gave her the opportunity to read *Bitch Nigga, Snitch Nigga* without being questioned by Q.

When she saw it at the airport, she'd acted like she was browsing through the magazines, but instead, she lifted a copy of it.

Red now understood what the hype about the book was all about and it gave her enough ammunition to get Bacon back for what he did to her.

The beginning of their second week, Q opened the door to Red's room, carrying a tray of sliced mango, pineapple and other exotic fruits along with fresh squeezed orange juice and whole grain toast. Red stirred when she heard the sound of footsteps approaching.

"Hey, sleepyhead," he said softly.

Red glared up at him, then threw her head up in the air and turned her back to him.

The attitude he was greeted with let him know she was still upset that he turned down her sexual advances, but she'd get over it, he thought. In spite of her cold shoulder, Q set the tray down in front of her, sat on the edge of the bed and turned her to face him. He hand-fed her a piece of fresh mango.

At first Red refused to open her mouth, but Q persisted. "C'mon, Red. You know how you love mango."

In spite of her pride, Red finally gave in and opened her mouth. The mango was scrumptious—a richer taste than the ones she'd eaten in the States.

"What are you doing up so early?" Red glanced over toward the clock. It was six in the morning. She chewed and swallowed the ripe piece of fruit as she waited for Q's response.

"Let's go sightseeing," Q suggested eagerly. "I bought you some clothes." He got up and retrieved a bag he'd left at the door. Red sat up in the bed and watched as he pulled out several swimsuits, shorts, halters, sundresses and sandals out of the bag and placed them on the bed. "I was thinking we could go snorkeling and horseback riding and take a tour to—"

Red put up her hand. "Stop!" she said forcefully, causing Q to step back. "First, you act like you want to be with me, then the next you don't. You reject my advances, now you're acting like nothing has ever happened." She glanced at the sun that was now in full view over the horizon and looked back at Q.

"Under normal circumstances, I'd even go with how you've been treating me, but look at me," she said, pointing to her face, "my face is fucked up. I can't go out looking like this."

Q understood what she was saying and she was right. Her face was still disfigured so he didn't press the issue any further. He walked over to Red, kissed her on the forehead and left. Red watched as Q closed the door behind him and a lump formed in her throat as she got out of bed and walked to the large glass patio door.

"It's beautiful," she said, sliding the door to the right and sauntered out onto the patio. Red gazed toward the semi-calm waters and tried to count the various shades of indigo. Looking at the white sand, she noticed how untouched it looked, as if nobody had ever set foot on it.

The palm trees held hammocks for rest and relaxation. Looking up at the clear sky, which was sprinkled with light white clouds like soft cotton, she saw seagulls fly and land on the water, flapping their large wings, making sounds that only seagulls knew. Red realized if she weren't in paradise, this was the next closest thing. With tears forming in her eyes, she went back inside and instantly became angry: as she walked past the full-length mirror on her way to the bathroom, an ugly image caught her attention. The black-and-blue marks were still there and the splint was beginning to get dirty from the constant wear. "I hate you, Bacon! I hate you!"

CHAPTER 8

*W*hile Red fumed in the bathroom Q took a walk on the beach. Walking and enjoying the sand under his feet, he asked himself, "Why can't I get her outta my system?"

He continued to hike along the beach. The warm waters washed ashore, covering his feet, then retracting. He was so consumed in his thoughts that he didn't hear his cell phone ring. The caller was persistent and called again. Q snapped out of his thoughts and answered it without looking at the caller ID. "Yo, wha'sup?" he said smoothly into the phone.

"Nigga, where yo' ass at? I'm hearin' shit that you got shot at, then I get a fat-ass check delivered at the crib from you and you ain't been answerin' yo' phone. Tell a nigga something," Zeke demanded.

"It's a long story, but everything is cool."

"Nah, nigga, who I gotta stop out here?" Zeke said seriously. "I can round up the old crew and handle business."

Q thought about it for a minute. He needed to get a location on Bacon.

"You heard of that nigga, Bacon?"

"Bacon? You mean that nigga that bitch Red used to fuck wit'?"

"Yeah, that's him."

"I'll see what I can find out, man. He been gone a minute."

"Well, he out."

"What?" Zeke said, shocked. "I ain't know his ass was home. I'll see what I can find out though."

Q became silent while he put his hand on his back pocket. He retrieved his wallet, looked inside and thumbed through his cash. "Hey, can you Western Union me about ten grand?"

"Ten grand?" Zeke raised his voice in disbelief. "What the fuck you need ten grand for?"

"I'm running low on funds. Red—"

"Red?" Zeke yelled into the phone. "She's with you?"

"Man, don't start. Like I said, it's a long story and I'll tell you about it when I get back." Q didn't want to hear what Zeke had to say. Then he remembered why Zeke was so bent on Red. "I know she fucked you over, but don't worry, man, Red will repay you."

An uncomfortable silence consumed the cellular airwaves until Zeke finally spoke up. "You'll have it within the hour." He ended the call before Q could say anything else.

"Yeah, she'll repay me," Zeke repeated as he drove to Western Union, "one way or another."

CHAPTER 9

"Come here, baby," Mekel said, flashing his sexy smile as he lay naked across their king-size bed.

Terry crawled into bed at his command. Mekel was met with soft warm kisses on his toes and her tongue traveled upward to the tool she longed for. Expertly, just as he had always liked it, she took him in and bathed his erection in warm saliva. They locked eyes as she served him. Mekel's dick seemed to take on a new life as he watched her take all of his length and width. When she thought he couldn't get any harder, he surprised her with even more girth. Mekel threw his head back and grabbed the back of her head with his left hand as he began to feel the tingling sensation inside his balls. He tried mightily to suppress the nut he wanted to release. It just wasn't time yet. He looked at her as she slowed down her pace and removed her mouth.

Their energy spoke volumes as she removed the towel from around her body and straddled him. Mekel suckled as hungrily as a newborn baby at her breasts while her hands explored his muscular chest and sculpted arms. She eased down on his shaft and they began to rock in rhythm of the motion that only they knew. She knew how to work her pussy to the fullest to pull out everything he had to offer. As they both were nearing an explosive climax, Mekel leaned forward forcing her back on the bed. His left arm automatically brought up her right leg as he could no longer control himself.

"You feel dat dick, baby?" he grunted with each down stroke.

"Yeah, Daddy, I feel that shit. Ooh . . . ooh . . . It feels . . . soo . . ." she screamed in rhythm to his thrusts.

"You ready for this . . . you ready for this?" His thrusts became more forceful and he was unable to hold back.

After what seemed like a series of never-ending orgasms, he collapsed on top of her.

He felt a nudge on his shoulder. "Mekel, you all right?" She nudged him again. "Mekel."

Mekel woke from his sleep and saw Kera looking back at him as she clutched her Bible. "Huh?"

"You've been tossing and turning for a while. Are you okay?"

Mekel was out of breath and his face dripped with sweat. The memory of the dream began to subside. Mekel felt wetness upon the sheet and began to fidget his legs to hide the evidence of his wet dream. "Yeah, I'm okay. I'm sorry if I woke you." He yawned.

A wail came through the baby monitor loud and clear. "I'll go get him," Kera told Mekel. She got up out of the bed and walked toward the nursery.

Man, Mekel said to himself, *what the hell?* He hurriedly changed his boxers then trotted down the hallway toward the nursery in an attempt to clear his memory.

Almost two weeks had gone since Terry tried to kidnap their newborn son, and Kera was trying her best to settle into her new role as a mother and a girlfriend. Ever since the incident, she went to church every chance she could and prayed daily for the health of their son.

Out of guilt, Mekel took over the diaper change once he got to the nursery. Kera stood next to him watching her two men.

"What—" he asked, quizzically. "What is this?" He rubbed his hand over his half-naked son. "Kera, why is he so greasy?"

"That's holy oil, Mekel. I blessed him."

Mekel reached for a wipe on the changing table; he heard a thud and saw the bottle on the floor.

"Kera, this ain't no damn holy oil," he said, picking up the bottle. "This is some extra-virgin olive oil."

"It was the closest thing I could find, baby. Don't worry though, I prayed over it and the Lord is blessing our lil' angel right now."

Mekel shook his head and put his focus back on his son. Kera loved watching him care for their son. He was as skilled as a marksman, but had the gentleness of a baby's touch when it came to his namesake. The once-scrawny newborn was now beginning to take on a healthier look. His skin tone was beginning to even out and his curly hair looked full. He still had the same eyebrows, almost connecting, that made him unmistakably Mekel Jr. The chubby cheeks he now sported was surely a sign of a healthy baby. Mekel was pleased with his progress.

"There. All done," he said to lil' Mekel. "Here baby, take care of this for me." He handed Kera the soiled Pamper. Kera shook her head, smiled and playfully tapped Mekel in the head with the bundled-up diaper, then disposed of it.

Fatigued, they both walked back down the hallway to the bedroom. Mekel absentmindedly slid into bed and pulled the covers back for Kera to join him. Instead, she assumed the prayer position on her side of the bed.

Please forgive me for all of my sins and those who have sinned against You as we know not what we do, she said silently. After that prayer, she spoke out loud. "Lord, thank You for the blessings You have bestowed upon me. Father God, please continue to watch over my family and we will forever serve You for the rest of the days of our lives. Amen."

A calm washed over Kera as she slid into bed next to Mekel and went to sleep.

Kera blinked and her eyes finally focused on the red LCD readout on the digital clock that was on her nightstand. Her eyes grew large as she read 8:49 A.M. She had slept for eight hours without being disturbed.

"Oh, my God, the baby!" she said out loud. She picked up the nursery monitor and held it close to her ear. She didn't hear anything. She kept the monitor inside the crib so she could hear the tiny baby breaths lil' Mekel made, but now, there was nothing but silence.

Kera's heart raced as she got out of bed and quickly walked out of their room and down the hall toward the nursery. Kera's heart trotted, doing Olympic-type somersaults in her chest. Her palms turned sweaty and she began to hyperventilate. Once inside the nursery she looked inside of the crib. Her eyes widened and her mouth formed a big "O."

"Mekel!" she yelled frantically as she turned around and rushed out of the nursery. "Mekel!" She ran back down the hallway, past the bathroom, past their bedroom and made a right down another short hallway, which led to the kitchen.

She stumbled into the living room and stopped in her tracks as she exhaled. A small tear dripped from her worried eyes. In front of her on the couch lay Mekel; and their son, swaddled, lying on top of Mekel's chest. They were both sleeping peacefully. If anything were a Kodak moment, this would be. Having been scared out of her mind, thinking that her baby had died, or was once again a victim of kidnapping, didn't sit well with Kera. Now her reaction was setting in.

She went to the bathroom and sat down on the toilet. "Damn, I gotta get myself together," she said as she felt the warm liquid escape her bladder. After a quick shower, Kera stood at the basin, wrapped in a plush, burgundy towel. She opened the medicine cabinet to retrieve her toothbrush and toothpaste. There was a bottle of Vagisil, which wasn't hers. Kera scowled. *I've been here for almost two weeks and it still doesn't feel like home. Everywhere I look this heifer's shit is in my face! Lord, please forgive me.*

She tossed the bottle into the trash and it landed with a small clinking sound. She looked at the towel she was wrapped in and immediately thought about Terry being wrapped in the same towel. Everything in the apartment reminded her of the past. Nothing was hers and she was sure Terry had something to do with how it was decorated. *Shit ain't even coordinated.* Kera began to visualize the décor throughout the apartment. Angrily, she stormed out of the bathroom and bumped into Mekel.

"Baby, what's wrong?" he inquired, seeing her panic.

"Nothing," she barked.

"Baby, for real, what's up?" He grabbed her arm gently as she tried to walk past him. "You've been uptight the last coupla days."

Mekel held her in his arms and smoothed her hair with his right hand.

As she allowed him to embrace her, Kera's angst began to subside. "Mekel, I thought it would be easy living here, but it's not."

"Wha . . . what you mean?"

"Everywhere I turn, I think about her."

"Who?" Mekel asked innocently.

"Terry!" she yelled like he should know and pushed away from him. "I'm sleeping in the same bed she slept in, I'm using the same towels and I'm wiping my ass with the same toilet paper she used. You have Cottonelle, I buy Charmin. It's too many memories here . . . too many of them of the woman who tried to kidnap our child."

"Kera, I understand, but you've been over here before. What's different now?"

"The difference is, we were just fucking, oops, having sex"—she looked up toward the ceiling and asked for forgiveness—"and there was no real idea that we'd be together. You weren't with me the majority of my pregnancy, but that's changed. We're a family now."

She had wanted to get with Mekel from the first time she saw him, but she let it pass because she knew his girl, Terry. But Mekel's reputation was known all over town—and so was his sexual prowess. Terry only validated it when she gave a very graphic, stroke by stroke account of his skills one evening when they were all chillin' at Red's.

Tired of all of the no-good niggas she encountered, Kera began to make herself known to Mekel just in passing. Although both were attracted to each other, neither acted on it until they ran into each other in Vegas and succumbed to the temptation of "What goes on in Vegas, stays in Vegas."

Kera knew that Mekel had broken up with Terry right before he left for Vegas; however, once they returned, things were different and Kera was left looking stupid: Terry and Mekel were back together and she, unbeknownst to her, had a baby brewing.

When Mekel learned of her pregnancy he was pissed, cut her off and denied the child. And, because of this, Kera fucked around with some of the niggas she kept on the side for extra ends. The looming pregnancy was something she didn't think about seriously. She at first thought, out of sight, out of mind; however, the choices she made would be ones that she would have to live with for the rest of her life.

Whenever they would run into each other, Mekel acted like he hated her. She played along with his fuck-a-ho, leave-a-ho ways. Kera couldn't lie to herself, though; she had feelings for him, and she played her cards just right. She didn't hound him . . . and he came right back to her, just like she knew he would.

"You're right, we *are* a family now, but what do you want me to do?"

Kera walked swiftly to the living room as he followed behind her. "I want to redecorate," she said with a smile. "First, I want to paint. This room would look great in lavender with white trim. Then we can get rid of all of this," she said, pointing to all of the furniture. She walked to the bedroom. "And see, close your eyes, baby, and visualize," she said excitedly. "We need another bed. I have one in mind." Kera was talking a mile a minute. "The chest is old and I can make—"

"Whoa . . . whoa . . . whoa," Mekel protested. "We don't need anything new. I just bought all this stuff a little over a year ago. There's nothing wrong with anything in here." He was becoming irritated.

Why can't he get over it? she asked herself. *Is Terry still on his mind? Is this a way to hold on to her? What about me?* Kera studied the expression on Mekel's face. She sighed deeply, trying to formulate her words.

Mekel looked at Kera then walked toward the bedroom window to peer outside. "I don't know, Kera, I just—" As he turned around, she dropped the bath towel she had wrapped around her. And walked toward him slowly.

"You don't know what, Mekel?" Kera stood up on her toes and kissed him.

"We can't," he protested.

Kera brought his hands up to her breasts. They were swollen and heavy, but Mekel couldn't resist the feel of them. He lowered his head to taste the left breast as he gently massaged the right with his hand. Not minding the release of breast milk, he lapped it up happily as if he needed it for nourishment. She reached down and felt his manhood peeping out of the opening of his boxers. Kera lifted her left leg up and placed the flat of her foot on the windowsill right behind Mekel. She then took his penis and ran it along the crack of her pussy, letting him feel how moist she was. Not caring how long it had been since she had given birth, Kera was going to use what got him away from Terry—her pussy. "Make love to me."

Mekel picked her up and carried her over to the bed. "You sure it's okay?" he asked against his better judgment.

"Yes, I'm sure," she reassured him as she guided him inside.

Although awkward at first, they found a groove they both enjoyed. Mekel was glad to be back inside of Kera's warm crevice and she was glad to accommodate his needs.

Twenty minutes later, they lay back on the bed, spent and out of breath.

"Mekel, I'm sorry," Kera said quietly. "It was wrong of me to ask you to get rid of your stuff. It's just hard to live behind another woman. Not only another woman, but a woman who hurt our son. That's it." She lowered her voice to a whisper. "I'll get over it." Kera wiped a fake tear from her eye.

Mekel watched her. He could see how much living in Terry's shadow was bothering her.

"There's no need to apologize. I should have taken care of this way before now. I know we can't erase the past, but if redecorating is what you want to do, then we'll do it. Go get your clothes on and I'll get the baby ready. Looks like you got a job to do."

Kera smiled as she layered kisses all over his face. *That was easy. Out with the old, in with the new. Thank you, Jesus.*

He smacked her on the ass as she jetted away to change, hoping he was doing the right thing.

CHAPTER 10

*M*aurice, a couple of his teammates and Bacon climbed off the plane in Cancun, and began walking toward baggage claim. Out of nowhere, children, young and old, immediately bombarded them, asking for autographs.

"Mr. Clarence! M. C.!" someone shouted.

"There's Tony!" a teenaged girl shrieked. "I can't believe it's you!"

"Kavaughn!" a young boy shouted. "You're my hero!"

The men graciously signed notebooks, shirts and shoes, and posed for pictures as Bacon blended into the swarm. Never one to be envious of others, he looked at them, and then himself. There was an obvious difference.

As the crowd dispersed, Maurice looked around for his friend. Understanding the perplexed look on his face, Maurice playfully boxed toward him.

Instinctively Bacon playfully blocked Maurice's punches.

"Come on, man," Maurice chided Bacon and draped his arm over his shoulder, "let's go get our luggage and change."

Just then, a group of women switched and swiveled their hips up to them. The men knew instantly that they were groupies by the overt sexual promiscuity they exuded. All four of them looked like local skeezers. From thick to bone-thin, short to tall, raven-colored to blond hair, each woman had her own look but seemed to be wearing the same uniform: painfully high stilettos, short miniskirts and tube tops so tight it looked as if their breasts were being massaged.

"Welcome, papi," the tallest one of the four said to the men. She turned around and did the bend-over-and-show-'em-my-ass routine. The guys didn't seem too put off by it, because she wasn't wearing any panties, and from what they saw, her pussy was fat.

The guys knew that whatever they asked for the women would allow it to go down. They were practically in the airport, fucking them. Each man walked away with a woman on their arm, Maurice with the fat-pussy one. The thick woman was left, and she looked at Bacon strangely.

"What's your name?" she asked, trying to make conversation. She knew just by looking at him he wasn't a ballplayer.

"Bacon," he said with the mack in his voice. "What's yo' name?"

"What kinda name is that?" The woman spoke English in a broken accent, ignoring his attempt to get hers.

"It means I got the bacon, you know . . . cash." Bacon motioned like he was rubbing money in between his fingers.

"Papi, if you gotta do all that," the woman said, irritated, realizing she got the runt of the bunch, "then you ain't sheit."

Bacon couldn't believe what she had just said to him. No woman had ever spoken to him in that tone before. Bacon's blood pressure began to rise. Red had shitted on him, and now

this bitch was telling him to his face he wasn't shit? Aw, hell naw.

Maurice heard what the woman had said and walked toward his friend, leaving the woman he was talking to standing alone. "All that ain't called for," he warned her. "You need to calm that shit down, mami."

Just minutes before he'd gotten off the phone with the Radisson Hotel after booking a suite for the night. He was about to get broke off. He didn't want this smart-mouthed heifer to block what was about to go down.

The feisty woman knew opportunity when she saw it, so she threw her hands up in surrender, and went along with the flow.

They were taken to the Radisson via limousine and retreated upstairs to the penthouse suite. Not long after hitting the door sounds of ecstasy filled the room. Nobody had shame in their game. It was one big orgy. Bacon watched on with a hard dick, as the woman who insulted him was doubling with one of Maurice's teammates. As she lay on her back getting pounded into, she looked at Bacon, licked her lips and mouthed, "You want it, don't you?" True enough, Bacon wanted it, but he knew that she was out of his league.

Bacon watched Maurice as he fucked Ms. Fat Pussy. Glad his boy was getting his, Bacon sulked to the bathroom and turned on the shower. Obviously upset that he couldn't get up in some pussy, he would handle his. He did before, and this wouldn't be any exception. As Bacon got into the shower and lathered himself, his hand instinctively went down to his thick erection. He closed his eyes as he went back in time.

"Bacon, what if we get caught? I'm scared."

"Don't be scared. The guard gave me some time. Stop playing."
He undid the zipper of her slacks, revealing her G-string. He turned

her around and admired her ass cheeks before spreading them apart. His tongue penetrated her asshole. Bacon rammed his thick dick into her pussy. He began to hump furiously, moving in and out with powerful thrusts. He was finally home again, in his bed, getting right.

"Don't come inside me," he remembered her saying.

"Too late," he said, grunting, as he shot his load in the shower. "Too fucking late."

Bacon's relief came at Red's expense. "In due time, we'll meet again," he said as he finished showering. He stepped out of the shower, dried off and went to bed, relieved. They had a big vacation day ahead of them.

Maurice and Bacon settled in at Maurice's off-season villa, nestled in the cut on Playa de Carmen. After showing Bacon the house he decided to hit the town. Maurice had some things he needed to do, and who else to do it with but his longtime buddy.

Maurice made a few calls as he drove toward the mainland. "Man, so how was them freaks last night?" Bacon questioned.

"You fuck one freak, you fucked them all." Maurice threw his head back and laughed.

As the two pulled away from Maurice's home, Bacon looked back. "Damn, you straight ballin'! Who would have thought?" he asked as Maurice drove away from the four-bedroom villa. "Yo' shit make my house look like a studio apartment." Both men chortled.

Maurice knew that his taste was extravagant but he also knew that Bacon was at the lowest point a man could be at in his life. He had nothing. All the stuff he worked hard for had landed him in jail; and even once he got out, he had nothing to go back to. No home, no family, no woman, no nothing.

"Do you believe in karma?" Maurice asked seriously.

"Yeah, what goes around comes around."

"Well, maybe we were supposed to meet up like this," Maurice rationalized. "Don't stress, you'll get back on your feet soon."

Maurice reached into his console, pulled out a toothpick and popped it into his mouth just as Bacon was about to ask how he figured that. Coming to his first location, Maurice parked the car and got out.

"It's nothing but a thing, man," Maurice assured him. "Come on. Follow me."

They walked through the entrance of Jose's. Jose was Maurice's favorite Mexican barber. He could cut the shit outta some hair. Mainly, black hair. Jose's was where the majority of the locals spent their time, imitating black hair, styles, walk and talk.

"Jose, my man!" Maurice greeted him with the customary one-arm hug.

"Ah . . . Reece, good to see you, mayne," he responded. "How's the knee?"

Maurice looked down at his long limb and nodded. "It's getting better. It's about eighty-five percent."

"Good," a patron chimed in. "Yo' team ain't shit without you."

"Damn right," another person said. "When you went down, they went down. All those damned rookies!"

Everyone laughed.

"Jose, this my main man, Is—"

"Bacon," he interrupted. Isadore was his middle name. His mother refused to call him by his birth name after his daddy left her. She said it reminded her too much of him.

"Any friend of Maurice's is definitely a friend of mine." Jose extended his hand for a handshake as he displayed a platinum grill. Bacon could do nothing but smile. This was your typical case of another ethnic group trying to be black.

"Hook my man up," Maurice said to Jose.

Jose snapped open the barber cape while Bacon sat down in the chair. Maurice watched as Jose worked his magic on his friend. About fifteen minutes later, Jose had trimmed Bacon's sparse facial hair into something that resembled the five o'clock shadow that women seem to love. Once Jose was finished, Maurice traded places with Bacon.

Bacon looked at the other patrons; they were smiling at him hard. It made him feel uncomfortable, like they were on some gay shit.

The door to the shop opened and in walked a familiar face. It was the woman who dissed Bacon the other day. He immediately became angry. As she walked into the establishment, she stopped and looked at Bacon.

"Ooh, papi," the woman purred. "Nice . . . real nice." She held eye contact with Bacon as she walked toward Jose.

Although angry, Bacon felt a familiar tingle in his dick as he thought about how she would look and feel riding him. He watched as she spoke to Jose in Spanish, then turned around and left. But before she left, she seductively blew a kiss at Bacon. He shook his head in disgust. *Women*, he said to himself, *just can't understand 'em.*

"There you go, my friend," Jose said as he finished Maurice's mustache.

Maurice flipped Jose a $100 bill. "Thank you as always." They pounded.

"You know you came just in time for the cruise, mayne. You know you always got a standing invitation."

Bacon was heavy in the game and knew what was up. He'd been on the cruise Jose mentioned with Red, Catfish and Sasha. Now he realized how Maurice really got down: although gone from the hood, he never truly abandoned the streets. His money gave him access to diverse investments and Bacon now knew why Maurice suggested the trip. Loyalty between ballers. Opportunity now was only a grasp away.

"I gotcha. We'll be there, man," Maurice confirmed.

CHAPTER 11

Q panted heavily as he made his way back to the resort. Just two hours ago, he left Red at the resort alone to retrieve the money Zeke sent. He was hotter than a muthafucka and wanted to get into someplace cool. He walked into quietness and saw a note on the glass table next to the door. Picking it up, he read:

> Q,
> *I can't continue to do this. It's not working, so I'm going to give you your space.*
>
> *Good-bye—Red*

He walked swiftly toward the room in which she was staying and saw her glide across the room, naked and shimmering with water. She had just taken a shower, and sat down on the bed to lotion her body. Watching her, he knew his heart was weak—the little head's voice was going to take over the situation. As she got

up to retrieve a pair of panties and a bra, she saw him study-
ing her.

"What are you doing here?" she asked, obviously shocked to
see him.

Q paused for a moment, taking in an eyeful of her body.
"What's the note about?"

She located a matching white lace set and stepped into the
panties and then hooked her bra. "Just what it says, I can't do
this anymore. I've already called a cab and I'm going to a hotel.
I've already booked my return flight, and it leaves in two days."
While Q was gone, Red had called Gloria, the only person she
could count on. Gloria was like the mother Red never had, and
in her heart, she knew that Gloria wouldn't let her down. Red
just hoped that Gloria would return her call before she made it
to the hotel, considering she had no money with her.

"You don't have to do that."

"I know I don't have to." She spoke firmly as she put more
clothes on. "But I can't stay with you feeling the way I do. You
hate me and I . . . I love you."

Over the last few days, Red realized that she truly *was* in love
and made the determination that she would change. She had to
change in order to keep her man, but deep down, she was tired
of being dirty. Dirty got her nowhere . . . she lost her baby, got
shot at and fucked up what she had with Q.

"You love me?" Q questioned. For some reason, the way she
said it sounded different than before. Like now, she actually
meant it.

"Yes," she confirmed. Just then a horn honked. "That's
my cab. You can keep the clothes. I don't need anything else
from you."

"Don't go," he said as she walked past him. Red continued to
head to the front door. Q walked quickly toward her as she

opened the door. He closed it. "I said don't go." She looked at him with tears in her eyes.

In one quick move, Q picked her up and carried her to the bedroom without removing his lips from hers. They explored each other's bodies, inside and out, like new lovers and they both realized this was where they wanted to be.

I can't let her go, Q confirmed to himself. *I love her. I can't play this game any longer.*

Looking into Red's face, he saw the beautiful woman that he loved. Her face was beginning to heal, but there was a softness in her he hadn't seen before.

"What's wrong?" Red asked. She noticed Q slowed his thrusts.

"Nothing, baby," he said as he stopped pumping. He wanted to cherish the sensation her pussy gave him while he was still. Red locked her legs around Q's back, and he resumed his movements.

"Baby, I'm sorry," he whispered in her ear. "I will never leave you again. I love you." Simultaneously the two climaxed. Q dozed off only to be awakened with warm kisses on his chest. He tried to move, but his energy was depleted. He wanted to take Red out and show her the island. She had missed a lot in their time there.

"We gotta get up," he said, still in a heavy pant.

"You are up," Red said with a sly smile as she stroked his member.

He looked down and smiled. "You're right."

Maurice took Bacon around to several exclusive boutique hotel spas in Playa del Carmen, which were about twenty-minute rides on the ferry. Bacon rejected his offer to go at first, but Maurice rationalized that Bacon had nothing in Mexico and this was the least he could do and he had the means to help. Maurice attempted to get Bacon accustomed to the finer things that legal money could buy. He owed a debt for his life and his career to Bacon, and they both knew it.

Bacon had heard men talk about being pampered with manicures, pedicures and facials and thought they had homo tendencies, but he had to admit the shit felt good. He wanted to put the thought out of his mind because of the times that he and Foxy fucked. It was okay, he rationalized to himself. She looked like a woman and felt like one as well.

The next stop was at a Rolex jewelry store. Maurice bought all of his jewelry in Mexico due to the wholesale duty free rates. The States taxed luxury items, but in Mexico, it was dirt cheap.

"You see something you like over there?" Maurice asked while trying to decide which watch he wanted to add to his collection. He noticed that Bacon was looking at something in the diamond case.

"You see these diamond studs over here? This is gangsta!"

"If you want 'em, get 'em. Remember, this is on me."

After paying for their purchases and leaving the jewelry store, the two walked past the Cartier store. Unable to resist, they both went in. Maurice bought a pair of shades for himself and bought Bacon a debonair pair of rimless, non-prescription glasses.

Their last stop was Maurice's personal tailor. He was always in suits except when he was on the basketball court. Maurice knew that image is everything so he was going to help Bacon with that—his image. He knew that dressing a certain way could get anyone just about anywhere.

"Where we going now?" Bacon asked. His stomach was growling and he was hoping they'd stop and get some food.

"You'll see," Maurice teased. "This will make you a new man."

"Ah . . . yeah, that's the shit," Bacon said, "you got a harem of hos and I get my pick, right?"

Maurice laughed at his friend. He felt bad because he didn't get any pussy the other night, but he was sure after what he had planned, pussy, or lack thereof, would no longer be a problem.

"Maurice, my main man!" the middle-aged Spanish man greeted when they arrived at the tailor's. "Welcome back!"

"Hey T, man, it's good to be back." T looked at the strange man who stood next to Maurice. "T, I'd like to introduce you to a longtime friend of mine, Bacon." Bacon outstretched his hand. "Bacon, this is my personal tailor, T." He took Bacon's hand and shook.

"Okay, let's get started," T suggested.

"Hey . . . hol' up, what are we starting?" Bacon asked.

"Getting you a new wardrobe. The stuff you're wearing is cool, but it's time to step ya game up."

T took Bacon's measurements and engaged in general conversation. Shortly afterward, Maurice and T were catching up, and Bacon noticed some suits that Maurice had hanging up. Even though he used to own designer suits, they were nothing of this quality. He took it upon himself to try one on, just on G. P.

Maurice glanced over at Bacon and stopped talking. T stopped as well when he saw Bacon. Both men grinned like school-age boys who saw a girl's tits for the first time.

"Fuck y'all grinning at?" Bacon said and walked over to the full-length mirror. He stood still, unable to recognize the man in the mirror. He moved his arm. The man in the mirror did the same thing, but Bacon couldn't believe it. "Damn," he said. "This me?" He looked like a new man and felt like one, too.

Maurice walked over to him, amazed at Bacon's transformation. "Now you know you can't walk around looking like a million bucks but calling yourself some swine. Good-bye, Bacon . . . Hello, Isadore Jeffries."

Bacon liked the sound of that. He looked like he had truly made it. Now nothing could stop him.

Red and Q decided to take a break from lovemaking. Their time on the island was slowly but surely coming to an end, so they filled their remaining days with numerous activities. Red's face and her nose had begun to heal and she was beginning to look like her old self again. With skillfully applied makeup, you couldn't see her scars at all.

As they began to wind down by relaxing on the beach, a young boy walked up to Q and handed him a box. Q handed him a $20 bill and the boy skipped happily away.

"What's this?" Red asked, opening up the box. Q didn't stop her. "Q!" she squealed. "You got it!"

Q surprised Red with a semi-sheer black Versace dress with a Chanel diamond-encrusted brooch at the waist.

Red excitedly tackled Q and planted kisses all over his face.

Q knew she wanted it when he saw her eyeing it, but he didn't buy it for her at that time. "You can wear that on the cruise coming up in two days."

"Cruise?" She acted surprised.

"The Dimes and Ballers Midnight Cruise," he reminded her. "You know, the one you've been bugging me about."

"You don't ball no more, Q," she reminded him.

"You right, but I still got connections."

The cruise was the biggest soirée for drug kingpins and their top generals to connect with other players in the major cities. Red hoped that Q would want to go. She figured if she could get him around the money again, he'd stop talking about getting out of the game. No matter how she felt about Q, Red needed the stash to maintain her lavish lifestyle.

When she mentioned it to Q, he flat out told her no, and no

amount of pouting would change his mind; but after he thought about it a little longer he realized that the game was all Red ever knew and he, as always, wanted to make her happy. Q couldn't take the game outta the playa, but began to wonder how their relationship would hold up without this lifestyle.

Red placed a tender kiss on Q's lips. She planned to thank him properly. She couldn't wait. Two days couldn't arrive soon enough.

CHAPTER 12

*T*wo days passed like a blink of an eye. The night of the Dimes and Ballers Midnight Cruise arrived.

After a day of sightseeing, Q and Red arrived back at the resort with not much time left to get ready. Earlier that day, they had visited the small village of Cedral and saw how the noncommercialized locals lived. Afterward, they enjoyed the El Cedral, which Red learned was the island's oldest ruins. Although she had visited before, she never knew the history of Cozumel; now she was truly able to enjoy the beauty, splendor and history the island had to offer. But tonight was all about the cruise.

Excitedly, Red held the black Versace dress that Q had surprised her with up to the mirror and envisioned herself wrapped in the delicate material.

"JLo ain't got nothin' on you, baby," Q joked. They both laughed. "But for real, though, let's get ready. We're already behind."

Red thought about his comment. Q was right. The dress he

had chosen put the famous blue-and-green, open-front Versace scarf dress that JLo wore to the Grammys to shame. Red knew that Q's bankroll ran long, and his taste was exquisite, and because of this, she was certain no other woman would come close to her tonight.

After bathing and lotioning, Red slipped into the dress and enjoyed the feel of the silky material against her skin. Q appeared in the doorway, dressed in a crisp, off-white linen suit, with a Cuban-style hat resting on top of his curls. *Damn*, Red thought as she saw him out of the corner of her eye. Q was looking good.

Q watched Red slip into her black, jeweled sandals and run her hand up the length of her leg. Once finished, she stood in front of her full-length mirror and admired how she looked. Q appeared behind Red and embraced her. He planted tiny kisses along the side of her neck.

"Ummm . . ." Red moaned as her right hand instinctively made its way up to the nape of Q's neck. "We look good together." Red closed her eyes to savor the moment and nestled against Q's body.

Q glanced at the clock. "Come on, baby." He took her hand and escorted her outside to the awaiting limo. When the two arrived at the drop-off point, they were amazed.

"Do you see this!" Red exclaimed.

"What?"

"Look at the yacht! It's tight!"

"Mm-hmm." Q nodded his head coolly, trying to play hard.

"And look at all the people, Q!"

Q glanced out of his window and saw the crowd. The driver got out of the car and opened the passenger's side door. Q stepped out and held out his hand, and Red slowly emerged.

Whistles could be heard from the crowd of spectators that formed on both sides of the security line. Security henchmen were in force because these were major players in the drug game.

Nothing ever popped off at this event and they were positioned to make sure nothing would. Red and Q boarded the yacht like royalty. White lights outlining the watercraft's upper and main decks sparkled like diamonds.

Mexican and Caribbean music filled the air. The majority of the men wore linen suits—some in white, others in black and a few in off-white.

Out of the one hundred travelers, Q spotted some of his former connects. Red noticed that quite a few of the women thought that "couture" meant dressing only in designer labels. Not only were they misled, they had no grace or style about them whatsoever. Red and Q, however, were poised and dressed such that they commanded respect. Nobody would have guessed that Q was getting out of the game and Red had just been pistol-whipped almost to death only two weeks earlier. Although still faintly bruised, she looked like a million bucks.

Q excused himself to get drinks just as the yacht began to set sail. Red walked further onto the main deck. The party was just beginning, but Red peeked in another room where three tables were heaped with food. On the first she saw huge platters of pineapple, mango, strawberries and papaya. Her eyes went to the next table and saw a silver platter piled high with lobster tails, tiger prawn shrimp and raw oysters. On the third were mounds of plantains, chicken, rice and peas and filet mignon on top of warmers. *Whoever is behind this,* she thought, *their money runs deep.*

Red went back onto the main deck and walked toward the balcony and looked out over the black, still water, waiting for Q to return. It was a clear night with a slight breeze; millions of stars sparkled in the sky. Red leaned against the railing and looked upward. She overheard people below talking about money, cars and celebrity gossip. She could do nothing but smirk at the show-offs.

If you gotta brag about it, you ain't 'bout it, she thought. The smell of new money was thick and she silently prayed that she wouldn't run into anyone she had played in the past or who knew her through Bacon. The thought put butterflies in her stomach.

Red strolled away from the balcony as a couple headed her way.

The handsome, dark-skinned man affectionately caressed the woman he was with, giving most of his attention to the growing bulge in her tummy. Red smiled at them as they walked by but a small tear formed in the corner of her eye as she thought back to her own pregnancy. Red's hand went to her flat stomach and she rubbed it slightly. Anger toward her mother's sexually abusive husband, Jerome, spiked inside her.

Red thought back to Bacon and the thoughts of revenge she had planted in him as to how she lost "their" baby. How Jerome had kicked it out of her. Would he avenge his baby's death?

"Them muthafuckas jumped me," she'd lied to him. *"So whatchu gon' do to dat muthafucka?"*

Red knew that once she told Bacon what had happened, he would take care of everything, including Jerome's pedophile ass. She just wondered if Bacon's anger with her would prevent him from handling the situation. If he didn't it was okay. She wanted to be the one to handle Jerome—*and* her mother. A hand slipped around her waist, startling her. She turned to see Q holding their drinks.

"You all right, baby?" Q asked, detecting that Red seemed uncomfortable.

"Yeah, I'm fine. I was just waiting for you." She took her long-stemmed glass from Q's hand and sipped at the golden bubbly liquid.

"All right," Q said hesitantly, "let's go kick it."

• • •

Throughout the night, Q mingled with some of the heavy hitters, while Red politely stood near him as his showpiece. Some of the women attempted to include Red in on their conversations, but she avoided talking about herself. Her evasiveness came across as being stuck up, so the other women went elsewhere. Q noticed this happening quite often, so he excused himself from the conversation he was having to talk to Red.

"Baby, come here," he said as he gently touched the small of her back and escorted her to a quiet place. "What's wrong? It doesn't look like you're having a good time."

"Baby, I'm having a great time." Red finished off her drink. "I just don't deal with too many women. Especially ones I don't know." She revealed her true feelings about her last girlfriends. "All my so-called friends were users—Sasha, Terry and Kera—and I'm just tired of the whole mess. I don't want to make any new friends."

Q nodded with understanding. "Red, I know you've been through a lot, but not everyone uses people. Don't let past experiences get in the way of making new ones." He caressed her cheek with his thumb. "Come on, baby." Q slowly led Red back to the group he was talking to. "Plus, you don't know these women and they don't know you. Half of them lyin' anyway." He tried to make light of the situation and Red smiled at his attempt.

"Hey, Q, my man!" a short Mexican man interrupted them. "You havin' a good time?"

"A wonderful time," Q admitted with a wide smile.

"And who is this lovely lady over here?"

"Jose, this is my girl, Raven." She extended her hand. "Baby, this is the man that made tonight possible." Jose took her hand and kissed it.

"This is very nice," she said, looking around. The rule of the game was never show a major playa that you're too impressed. Too much excitement shows that you never had shit.

"Q, why don't you come up top later?" Jose motioned toward the upper level. "I think you and your lady friend may like the view." He had heard in conversations of a new product, in various forms, that could make anyone in the game an instant millionaire. Although Q was trying to get out of the game, his curiosity was getting the best of him.

"A'ight, bet," Q confirmed. "We'll be checkin' you out later."

Red and Q walked away and blended into the crowd.

Red took Q's advice and mingled with the men and their women. After a few hours, she realized she was enjoying herself. Most of the conversation revolved around being wifey, expensive shopping sprees, exotic vacations and, of course, major loot.

Red remembered her introduction into the wifey lifestyle, courtesy of Blue, and some of her other conquests. However, Bacon had been her biggest score, and truth be told, she had enjoyed her opulent lifestyle. *Too bad he wasn't able to enjoy it after he got locked up, because I sure did have a ball.* Red smiled a sinister grin at the thought.

Meanwhile, on the upper deck, another party of sorts kicked off. These were the major players of the dope game and long-term connections had been made. Bacon's newfound confidence and appearance allowed him to network in a way he never had before. He realized that his street persona would only allow him to get so far. Now, it was a whole new day.

"Papi, you wanna taste this?" Maria, the thick one, asked Bacon. She finally gave up a name and was trying her best to entice him while she attempted to feed him a tiger prawn. "It's big and juicy," she purred, taking a seat on his lap and grinding her ass into his crotch.

Bacon knew exactly what she was up to. *Bitch ain't want me at first, now she ridin' my joint. These women ain't good for nothin' but fuckin'*. He thought back to Red and was humiliated because he'd been played by her all along. First her, now Maria was standing in his face, trying to serve pussy on a platter.

"So now you want some of dis, huh?" Bacon asked.

"Papi, I want all of it." She gyrated some more.

Bacon couldn't help but get an erection. He hadn't had pussy since Foxy and it was past time to get up in the sweet gushy, but now wasn't the time. He had business to take care of.

Bacon spotted Jose talking to Maurice and some other people. He excused himself and left Maria, who was shocked to be denied.

"Isadore, my main man!" Jose greeted him. "You enjoyin' yourself? Is there anything I can get for you?"

"I have everything I could want and more," Bacon answered honestly.

"Good . . . good."

A beautiful, well-toned woman walked by them on her way back to the small pool. All of their eyes followed as her luscious ass bounced every time she took a step.

"Man," Jose said. "You think that's something . . . you might wanna go downstairs. There's one that puts all these women to shame."

"Straight up?" Bacon replied.

"Yeah. I'm sure she'll be up soon. Acts like none of this shit impresses her, but it does." The men knew her type very well. "When Raven comes up you'll see what I mean. She is what tonight is all about."

The men looked on in hopes of more.

Raven? A darkness washed over Bacon. He would have to go to the main level to see for himself, but in due time.

Bacon spent his time networking and now had enough connections to get him back on top and never fall. He wanted to get to the main deck to see this Raven person Jose referred to earlier, but he had more important matters at hand. When Bacon first met Jose, he didn't realize the barbershop was a cover for his drug ring.

There was something about Bacon that Jose liked . . . his pride, his determination, but mainly his hunger. Jose figured by allowing Bacon to work for him, they'd both benefit from it.

Maria stayed close by Bacon's side all night, making it harder to turn down her advances. Half drunk and having had some Black Tar heroin, Bacon was sure he would take her back to Maurice's villa and beat the walls out of her pussy. *I don't care how good this shit is*, he vowed as peered at Maria, *I will never let another woman stand in the way of, or benefit from, my come-up.*

Once the cruise came to an end, Q escorted Red back to their waiting limo. On their way to the resort, they couldn't keep their hands off each other. The alcohol they'd consumed took over their bodies, making every sensation more pronounced.

"Q, baby," Red said between kisses, "thank you."

"For what?" he asked with her breast in his mouth and his hand caressing her thigh.

Red couldn't concentrate enough to answer him. The limo

arrived at their destination. Q quickly helped Red become presentable before the driver opened the door. Once they were back in their room, they hurriedly undressed each other and made love where their clothes landed. After the first climax, Q carried Red to the bedroom and laid her across the bed.

"What were you saying earlier?" Q asked. "You said thank you. Thank you for what?"

"Just being here for me. I know these last two weeks weren't what you wanted, but I've realized that I've taken you for granted and to be honest with you Q, it was just a facade. I was afraid of being hurt, but I now know you won't hurt me."

"I would never do that, Red."

"I want to be with you, Q." She looked at him in his eyes. "I want to take this farther and see where it goes. Do I still have a home once we get back to Detroit?" Red was referring to the loft she'd conned Q into buying.

"It wouldn't be home without you."

Red and Q regained their energy and made love repeatedly throughout the night. Their fantasy would be over in just a few hours. It was time to return home . . . back to reality.

$\mathcal{S}$h . . ." Kera put her fingers to her lips as Mekel peeked in on her and the baby. Mekel wondered why Kera always seemed so stressed nowadays. He figured it was because she was back at work from her maternity leave and was tired. He made sure he got up in the middle of the night when lil' Mekel woke up so she could get her rest. He did everything she asked of him, and then some, so he wondered why Kera wasn't happy now. After all, she had her baby back safely, she had redecorated and she'd even gotten her baby's father to leave his woman for her—something Mekel never thought he'd do in a million years . . . wind up with Kera. He watched her go into the bedroom and followed behind her.

She eased the baby into his crib and dragged herself toward their bedroom and dropped like a rag doll.

"Waa . . . sniff . . . sniff . . . waa!" the baby bellowed again.

"I'll get him." Mekel rubbed Kera on the back, then headed back toward the nursery. *Why does he have to cry so much?* he said to himself. Arriving in front of the crib, he reached down and picked him up firmly, hoping Kera hadn't blessed him again.

"A'ight, lil' man." Mekel held him so close to his chest, he could hear his baby's heart beating. He grabbed a changing pad and sat down in the glider, spreading the pad on his lap. Talking to him in baby talk, he laid his son on his lap and checked his diaper.

"Aw . . . that's the problem," he cooed as he discovered the smelly, soft mush. After he cleaned Mekel Jr. up, giving him a fresh powder and diaper, Mekel kissed his son's tiny feet, suddenly realizing what that one crazy-ass night in Las Vegas created. He was elated that he was now a father and to him, his son was perfect. No one could tell him anything different. He grabbed a receiving blanket and swaddled his son tightly. He noticed that when the baby was wrapped tightly, he didn't seem to cry so much, something that he was certain that Kera didn't know.

He walked to the window and gently massaged his son's back. "Don't worry, lil' man. Daddy got you." With that, he went to the living room and lay down on the couch with his son on his chest, where they both went to sleep . . . peacefully.

Kera overheard Mekel's claim, "Daddy got you," through the baby monitor. She sucked in her trembling lips as tears escaped her eyes. How would Mekel react when she told him her secret? She'd never felt lower in her life.

Then the horrible truth hit her once again. How could her whole world turn from so bright to so dark in just one conversation with the doctor? Kera tried to make sense of the information she'd received from the pediatric neurologist the other day, all the while still battling nightmares of the kidnapping. It was just too many traumas, too close together; one onslaught after another had exhausted her, both mentally and physically. Somewhere in the back of her mind, even before the appointment, she knew her child wasn't out of the woods. Maybe it was her maternal instincts, but she knew there was a long road ahead of them.

Kera lay on the examining table while her OB/GYN spread the blue gel over small protrusion of her belly. She was just now beginning her second trimester. Her first trimester was challenging and she thought she would lose her baby. She didn't care at first because she didn't like how Mekel had played her.

Although Kera didn't have the amount of men that Red had, she did keep male company who kicked her some ends from time to time. Kera's displeasure with Mekel turned her into a woman even she didn't know. She kicked it, drinking, smoking weed and having wild sex. None of her partners knew she was pregnant because she was so small and not showing, but they said something was different with the way her pussy felt . . . it felt better. That kept them coming and cumming.

She realized as well that sex was better, and since she couldn't have Mekel, any dick would do. Only when she felt the first faint flutter in her stomach did she realize she was going to be someone's mother with or without Mekel. At that revelation, Kera stopped her promiscuous behavior and began anticipating her new arrival.

"There it is," the doctor spoke as he found the baby's heartbeat. "Nice and strong," he confirmed. The doctor handed Kera a wet wipe to clean herself off and sat down on the stool. He opened her chart and began to ask questions.

"How have you been feeling?"

"I've been feeling well."

"Good. I was concerned about you. You seemed upset the last time you were here."

"I guess I was just emotional."

"Any alcohol or drug use?"

"No," she lied.

"Unprotected sexual behavior?"

"Nooo!" Kera exclaimed, embarrassed.

"Just standard procedure," the doctor assured her. "Well, everything looks great. Schedule your next month's appointment before you leave and I'll see you in four weeks."

Kera's mind fast-forwarded to her most recent visit with lil' Mekel's pediatrician. They were joined by a pediatric neurologist. Kera brought the baby in because she didn't feel he was progressing as well as he should. At almost two months old, he should have been holding his head up, cooing and laughing. But he wasn't.

"Kera, I need to ask you a question," the pediatrician said to her, as she fastened the baby's diaper. "Did you drink or do drugs during your pregnancy?"

Tearful, Kera replied, "I did drink some but—"

"Well, your son has classic signs of fetal alcohol syndrome. The fine motor skills and developmental delay is the result of repeated alcohol use." The neurologist looked at her and shook his head.

Kera held tightly on to little Mekel, rocked back and forth and cried. "No, my baby can't be . . ."

She'd demanded a second opinion. *Delayed motor skills . . . mental delays that won't be noticeable until after the first birthday*, played in her head as she remembered what the doctor told her. Kera was brought back to reality listening to Mekel converse with their son over the baby monitor. *There's no way in hell that my baby is retarded*, she thought. *No fucking way!*

A couple of hours passed and Mekel bottle-fed his son, who was now wide awake. He couldn't continue to hold him, although he wanted to; he had to clean up around the apartment. Kera had seemed too depressed lately to keep the dishes washed, the place picked up or the clothes washed and folded, so he decided to do it himself. He hoped Kera didn't have that postpartum depression he'd heard about on *Oprah* once.

He unwrapped his son, placed him in the swing, and pushed the start button. He gazed on as his son gently swung back and forth, and listened to the lovely melody flowing from the music box. Suddenly his son's head slumped to the left and Mekel got a vision that made him shudder. He had seen that look on "special" children.

Mekel stopped the swing, and removed the infant headrest from the baby carrier and placed it behind his son. Even though his son was almost two months old, Mekel figured he wasn't old enough to hold his head up yet anyhow.

"That's better," Mekel said softly and started the swing up again. He watched for about a minute as his son enjoyed the swing. Then Mekel grabbed a load of clothes out of the hamper and sat on the couch, beginning to sort them to wash. He heard something hard drop to the floor as he separated the darks from the lights.

Seeing it was his cell phone he picked it up. The red light was flashing, indicating he had a message. He flipped it open. It read: *4 missed calls.*

Mekel dialed the number to check his voice mail; the first three calls were from women offering everything from money to sex. One even offered her home to him when he got tired of playing daddy. The last call was only a recording. Someone had tried to contact him from the county jail. His mind wandered a mile a minute. *I wonder who that could have been?* As he continued to sort the clothes, he assured himself, "They'll call back if it was important."

CHAPTER 14

A week had passed since Red and Q returned home. They lay low to give their bodies time to adjust to the climate change. Q headed out early to cruise the neighborhood. After driving around, he stopped at Foxy's. He rang the bell repeatedly, just to piss her off. He heard her cursing as she stomped toward the front door.

"What the fuck is your—" Foxy flung open the door and started to go off until she saw Q standing in front of her with a large grin on his face.

"Q!" Foxy squealed and stepped back to let him inside the house. Once she closed the door, they exchanged hugs. Foxy was elated and relieved to see him. She was glad to see that Bacon hadn't lied about not killing him. "So, where you been?" she asked, trotting off to the kitchen to get a beer. "I ain't seen you in a long time." She returned with the beer and handed it to Q, who took a seat in the living room. She raised an eyebrow and took in how good he looked. Actually, he looked better than ever with that sun-kissed skin.

"I been to Mexico," he replied then turned the bottle up to his lips and sucked down the golden liquid. "Needed a change of scenery." He plunked the bottle down on the coaster on the coffee table.

"Well, the change looks like it did you well." Foxy playfully kneaded his pectorals. "You look better than ever."

Q blushed and they spent the next half hour catching up. However, Foxy's smile diminished quickly when Red's name was brought up.

"Just spending this time with her," Q admitted, "I think we've come to a mutual understanding. I think I'm gonna try to make it work."

"What about Bacon?" Foxy quizzed.

"He's the least of my worries right now. But he definitely got something comin' his way," Q promised.

"Q." Foxy sighed, and carefully chose her next words. "I know you love Red, or you think you do. Because of this, I support you, but just be careful. She's not gonna change," she warned.

Q's demeanor changed and Foxy noticed it, so she quickly changed the subject. "Did ya hear that Black Tar is on the street?"

Still upset about what she had said about his relationship with Red, Q glared at Foxy, eyes slightly squinted. "It's supposed to be better than any of this other shit out here. Niggas trying to get it left and right, but it's hard to get."

Q thought back to the midnight cruise and the bells ringing over the drug. He knew what she was referring to. Anyone who was anyone spoke about it on the midnight cruise, but he was surprised it was in Detroit so soon. Q had to admit, getting back into the game with something as prime as this was tempting, but he was adamant about getting out. Q's mind quickly diverted back to the check Red gave him at the church. One point six million dollars was nothing to sneeze at, and if invested properly, that would be pocket change. Red told Q that she would deposit the check today. He was glad. He was ready to move on with the other phase of his life.

Q stood up. "Well, Foxy, c'mere, give me a hug."

Foxy complied. "When you gonna let me show you how a real woman does it?" she asked seriously.

"I don't think I can handle you." Q was amazed at how real Foxy's breasts felt against his chest. *If I didn't know she was a he, I'da fucked her a while ago.* "You're a whole lotta woman." Q laughed to clear his thought, and began walking toward the door.

"And don't forget that," Foxy joked.

Q headed back to the loft. He hoped Red was at the bank cashing the check he'd gotten back from Zeke the night before. It was time to move on with their lives.

Bacon sat in Maurice's new BMW 760Li sedan outside Foxy's apartment. He wanted to see her as soon as he got home because he wanted some pussy, but he saw a familiar Range Rover on the street, then saw Q leaving. A few minutes later, Foxy called his cell phone, but he didn't answer. He was too busy reflecting back to his last conversation with her. *Is he fucking her, too? I didn't know she knew him. I wonder what else she hasn't told me.* Bacon followed Q when he pulled away from Poindexter Village Apartments. He needed to get a location on Q—he knew Red wouldn't be that far behind.

Bacon sat in his car laying in the cut on Q. It was a perfect chance for him to do Q, but he wanted to find out where Red was first. Bacon watched as Q hugged an older woman good-bye. Bacon assumed that it was a family member, and now that he knew where Q's family was, he knew he'd always have a way to catch up with him again. Not wanting to be detected, Bacon slumped down in his seat a bit as Q drove right past him. Bacon pulled off in the opposite direction and circled the block one last time. *We'll see each other again,* he promised himself.

Later that evening, back in Bloomfield Hills, Bacon stewed that his home was no longer his. Although Maurice welcomed the company, it didn't sit right with Bacon that he was a guest in his own home.

Getting out of the car and gathering the mail, he went inside and sat down. After thumbing through it, he saw a letter from Triple Crown Publications addressed to Lisa Lennox. He tore into it and read:

> *Dear Ms. Lennox,*
>
> *Due to the overwhelming success of your novel,* Bitch Nigga, Snitch Nigga, *we would like to offer you another one-book deal worth $50,000. If this would be of interest to you, please contact me.*
>
> *Also enclosed is the second payment for the contract of* Bitch Nigga, Snitch Nigga *as well as royalties.*
>
> *Kammi Johnson*

Bacon looked at the checks that were included with the correspondence. The first one was for $15,000 and the second was for $10,000.

"Not bad," Bacon said, holding the checks worth 25 g's in his hand. He ambled to the telephone and called the phone number listed on the letterhead.

"Triple Crown Publications, how may I help you?"

"May I speak with Kammi Johnson?" Bacon code-switched and asked in his most professional sounding voice.

The person put Bacon on hold.

"Hi, this is Kammi. How may I help you?"

"This is Isadore Jeffries, agent to Lisa Lennox."

"Good morning Mr. Jeffries," Kammi replied cheerfully. "How may I help you?"

"I'm contacting you regarding the correspondence you sent pertaining to another contract. We'd like to get everything moving as fast as possible." Bacon smiled.

"Great, Mr. Jeffries. Uh . . . you said you're Lisa's agent, correct?"

"Yes. She's actually away on a personal family matter." He lowered his voice to get sympathy. "Her sister Raven was murdered."

"Oh, I'm sorry to hear that! We can wait, Mr. Jeffries, until she's able to talk to us."

"As her agent, I have proxy to sign whatever documents you need."

"Great. We'd like to get this going ASAP as well. Do you have a fax machine so we can send the contract?"

Bacon gave Kammi the number to the fax machine that was upstairs in Maurice's office.

A shit-eating grin plastered Bacon's face when he saw they were willing to pay 50 g's for the second book. Because they thought he had proxy, Bacon was able to sign the contract for Red.

Fair exchange ain't robbery.

Red arrived at the unusually crowded bank. She wanted Q to go with her but he elected not to. Always impatient, today she didn't let the crowd bother her. She was hopeful and ready to begin her new life with Q. She stood in line after filling out her deposit slip, waiting patiently for her turn. About twelve minutes later, she heard, "Next," and walked over to the next available teller.

"How may I help you?" the friendly voice behind the window asked.

Both women stood in shock for a minute. It was Kera! They hadn't seen each other since the move, a little over a couple of months. Red noticed that Kera looked tired and worn-out. Her hair was unstyled and she looked like the life was drained out of her. Red, on the other hand, was looking her best.

"I'd like to deposit this into my checking account."

As Kera's gaze took in the amount of the check her eyebrows rose instantly, making her amber eyes more pronounced. "As a matter of fact," Red added, wanting to rub Kera's nose in shit, "I'd like ten thousand back." She smiled.

Kera attempted to make small talk while she began to punch a bunch of numbers. "Checking or savings?" she asked out of habit.

"I said checking," Red said smartly. She didn't look Kera directly in the eye. She treated her like a mere customer service clerk, not like someone who was once her friend. Red would never forget how Kera had betrayed her and almost cost her her very life. If it wasn't for her sending that letter to Bacon, Red wouldn't be in the situation she was in now. She wouldn't have gone to visit him, she wouldn't have fucked him and the paternity of her baby would have been known. In a sense, Red was glad she didn't have the baby because she didn't know whose it was, but it was just the principle that Kera was supposed to have been her friend and fucked her in the end.

"Have you heard from Sasha?" Kera asked as she keyed in more numbers.

"I've been out of the country," Red said sarcastically.

"Well, girl, she got a new man, and it looks like he's taking good care of her."

"That's nice." Red began patting her foot, impatiently.

Suddenly, whatever Kera had punched in her computer made a beeping sound. Red drummed her perfectly manicured nails on the dark granite countertop. "What's taking so long?"

"She may still be in town." Kera began to key the numbers again. "I met the dude she's with." The numbering sequence caused another beep. "She said he had some business to tend to, but girl, he was the blackest nigga I have ever seen. I think that's what she called him too—Black." She paused for a moment. "Naw, it was Blue. Hey, I'll be back in a minute." She flounced away with Red's check.

Blue?! Inside, Red was fuming when she thought of Sasha being with Blue. Droplets of sweat formed on her nose. *That bitch always wanted to be like me . . . BE me. Now she with Blue? Even though I don't want his shit-mouth ass, he will* always *be my man,* she thought. She was going to track down Sasha to see if this was indeed true. For Sasha's sake, she prayed it wasn't.

Red abruptly came back to her senses when Kera returned to her window with the check and a small piece of paper.

"So, how's life as a new mommy treating you?" Red figured Kera was embarrassed with the way she'd let herself go. "How's the happy little family?"

"Actually, we're fine," Kera lied as she slid a picture of the three of them toward Red.

"Oh, wow," she said, fakely. "Isn't this sweet."

Kera began following the instructions on the piece of paper and slid the check through her machine. This time, it didn't beep. They both heard the machine imprint something on the check. Red was glad. She was ready to get out of there but not before hammering a nail in Kera's casket.

"You heard from Terry?"

Lord, please help me hold my tongue. Kera's eyes narrowed as she looked at Red, who was now grinning like she had won the lottery. *Fuckin' bitch*, she said to herself, then apologized to the Lord. She grabbed the check and read the printout. Her scowl was replaced with an even bigger grin than Red's.

"There's been a stop payment on this check," Kera said in a louder than normal voice.

"What? Run it through again!"

"I've done it three times. You may want to get in touch with the issuer." Kera continued to talk loudly so the other customers could hear. She smiled because she knew Red was embarrassed. "I'm gonna have to take thirty dollars out of your account for a returned check fee."

In a huff, Red grabbed the check. "Take it out!" She stomped out the bank.

Little did Red know that was all Kera needed for her to say because she had more plans to get back at Red: Fair exchange ain't robbery.

With a satisfied feeling, Kera called out, "Next!"

CHAPTER 15

*S*eeing Q made his mother smile. She had been worried about him because she hadn't heard from him in weeks and their last phone call had ended so abruptly. Q wasn't expecting her to come over. Although his mother was welcomed at his home any-time, he was glad she'd arrived after Red left for the bank. He didn't feel like any drama today.

Q's mother questioned him about his whereabouts and the reason behind his sudden departure, but Q never gave her a straight answer.

"Was it because of Raven?" she asked, her lips pursed. Q could never lie to his mother, so instead of starting, he didn't an-swer. She knew what that meant. "Q, you're a grown man, but I will always be your mother."

"I know, Mama." Q kissed her on the cheek in hopes to divert her thoughts.

His mother walked into the kitchen. "You'll never guess who I ran into while you were away."

"Who, Ma?"

Red was pissed off about the check when she got to the loft. When she heard voices, she closed the door as quietly as she could. Q and his mother were in deep conversation. She didn't alert them that she was home, she wanted to hear the rest of their conversation.

"Anyway, no woman will ever know you like I do," said Q's mom.

"You're right, Ma." He kissed his mother on her cheek. "And just so you know, no woman will ever take your place." He knew what his mother was getting at and he wanted to reassure her that she'd always be his number-one girl.

Red heard them walking toward the kitchen door. She ducked behind a partially built wall that held a flat screen TV. It shielded her from Q and his mother's view.

"Be careful, son," she said as Q escorted her to the front door. "I know a snake when I see one."

Red was beyond livid now. She knew that Q's mother didn't like her, but this was taking it too far. She was going to make Q's mother eat her words.

Q was always spoiling his mom, and they left to go to the mall. Soon Red was left alone in the loft.

Red paced around the apartment, trying to cool off. She'd come home to tell Q about the check, but knew that doing so immediately would cause more questions than she had answers for. She worried that the money, or lack thereof, would change their relationship, and that was not a question Red was ready to tackle. She decided to leave well enough alone until she received answers.

Watching the Channel 10 News, Red listened while the reporter told the Motor City how dumb Mayor Kilpatrick really had become.

"In the middle of the affair, the mayor texted love notes to his aide."

Red's mind quickly went back to Q's mother. She couldn't believe the woman called her a snake, especially considering she didn't even know her.

During the trip to Mexico, Red had made a conscious effort to begin to right the wrongs she had done to Q. It appeared as if she was still on the right path. Now she was afraid that Q's mother would distort his perception of her and open old wounds.

The words Q spoke to his mother lingered in her mind. She knew she could never take his mother's place, but she was gonna sure try. She was even more pissed that Q had left the house with his mother. Red continued pacing and stopped in front of the couch.

"Damnit!" she yelled, and swung her arms, knocking two pictures that were on the end table to the floor. Everything was going wrong all at once. She had also been trying to get in touch with Gloria for a couple of days and so far was unsuccessful. Red was so incensed about what was going on that she didn't hear the knock or notice the turning of the doorknob on the front door. Stomping toward the door, ready to leave to go to the office, she flung it open.

CHAPTER 16

*H*ey, baby," Kera said as she walked through the front door. She took a half day off to spend with Mekel. Mekel was able to make ten times the money Kera made, with fewer hours worked. His job as a hustler made her somewhat envious. Mekel would rise early to check his traps, and then spend the afternoons and evenings at home chillin'.

Lil' Mekel was in his swing, enjoying the ride, while Mekel was in the kitchen putting the finishing touches on lunch.

"Hey, ma," he greeted her.

She stopped the swing, picked up the baby and walked into the kitchen.

"How was your day?" he asked.

"You won't believe who came in the bank today."

"Who?"

"Red."

"Red?" Mekel had to search his memory bank. "Oh, your girl who you stayed with."

"Yeah, her. Well, guess what. You know she's a real estate agent, right? Well she comes in the bank today to cash a one-point-six-million-dollar check."

"O-kay."

"And there's a stop payment on it."

Mekel's eyes got big. "Ooh, that's messed up. I know that had to be embarrassing," he said after Kera told him how crowded the bank was. "I feel sorry for her."

"Feel sorry for her? For what?"

"That's your girl, isn't it?"

"Yeah, and."

"The fact that she tried to cash a check that large, she was obviously going to do something with the money. Man, that's messed up."

Kera looked at Mekel like he was crazy. She didn't want him to know why Red was upset with her or anything about their history. Kera wanted to maintain the pristine image that Mekel had of her. Her plan to take him away from Terry had worked. He just didn't know it.

After lunch and a relatively peaceful afternoon, Mekel was in the nursery about to put his son down for a nap and Kera was in their bedroom putting clothes away when the phone rang.

"I'll get it," Kera yelled. "Hello?"

An automated voice came through. "You have a prepaid call from"—*Terry*, another voice said. "Press five to accept or hang up to decline the call."

Kera pressed five. She had some stuff to get off her chest.

"Hello. Is Mekel there?"

Kera cocked her neck to the side and looked at the phone. *She got her nerve calling here for my man,* she thought. "Who is this?" she asked in order to taunt Terry. She had a major attitude.

"You know who this is, Kera."

Kera's blood pressure rose instantly. She wanted to yell, but decided against it. No need to alarm Mekel when she had something she needed to tell this crazy trick. All of the religion left Kera's body. She gritted her teeth and spoke forcefully. "Bitch, you got your nerve to call here."

"Look, I asked to speak to Mekel."

"Well, you gotta go through me to get to him, so whatever you have to say to him, you can say it to me."

There was silence on the other end. Finally, Terry spoke up. "Well, can you put him on the other phone? That way, I only have to say this once."

That was a reasonable request, but Kera wanted to add more salt to the wound. "Actually," she said through a yawn, "he's waiting for me in our bedroom." She paused for a moment to gather more venom. "Just so you know, Mekel is a great father, Terry. He said he wants to have a lot more kids with me," she lied. "By the way, how are your kids, Terry . . . and their fathers?"

Despite how much of a Christian Kera had become, she couldn't resist hitting Terry just where it hurt; she knew Terry had lost custody of her children and her baby's daddies were ghost.

"Okay, I deserve that, Kera." There was another light pause. "How's the baby?"

Kera pulled the receiver away from her ear and looked at it as if it were a foreign object. "Do you really care, Terry? You try to kidnap my baby, then you wanna know how he's doing? What? You wanna make sure he's okay so you can do it again?"

"Look, Kera, I was calling because I was wrong. I didn't mean to hurt you, Mekel and most of all, your son. I hope he's okay because if he's not, I would never be able to live with myself."

Kera fell silent momentarily. She actually felt sincerity in

Terry's words; however, this was something that would not go away with an apology.

"You know what, you just better be glad you're behind bars because that's the only place you're safe right now," she threatened. "Oh, and don't call back here. Mekel doesn't want to talk to you." She slammed the phone down. A voice behind her startled her.

"I don't want to talk to who?"

"Ooh, you scared me," Red exclaimed. When she'd flung open the door, it revealed Zeke standing there.

"Where's my money, bitch?" Zeke said.

"What money?" Red was caught off guard.

"Cut the bullshit," he demanded, pushing past her into the loft. "I know about the check you gave Q, and I've waited long enough."

She looked at him quizzically. Zeke knew what she was doing, but stopped her. "Don't play dumb with me." He walked up on her and coughed in her face. She could smell a strong alcohol stench coming from his pores. She now knew where he got his brazen attitude . . . he was drunk. "Since you got so much, I want six times what you owe me."

Red took a step back and put her hands on her hips. "Six?"

"You heard me, bitch. I ain't stutter. Fifteen for the money you owe me and fifteen for almost getting my man killed."

"What you gotta do with that?"

"I wired him money while y'all was on the run in Mexico. Thing is, bitch, my man don't run. He was tryin' ta protect yo' ass, so I want that, too . . . plus interest."

Red smiled and shook her head.

"Fuck you smiling for?" Zeke asked, angrily.

"The fact that you want me"—she pointed to herself—"to give you"—she pointed toward him—"thirty g's."

Zeke grabbed her wrists. "And I want it now." He looked at her and she jerked her wrists away. "If I don't get it now"—he narrowed his eyes then took his index finger and traced the outline of her breast—"I'll take something else, then tell Q you broke me off. I can always come back for the money."

"Broke you off? You outta your fuckin' mind! He won't believe that shit." She turned to walk away but Zeke pulled her to him and bit her on the side of the neck, hard.

She screamed, clearly stunned by his actions. "Get yo' hands off me!" she spat with venom.

Zeke's cell phone began to ring. He looked at the display and smiled. "Well, look what we have here," he jibed. "It's Quincy." He showed Red the caller ID. "I wonder how he would feel if I told him I was at his crib alone with you. He'd come home and see that big-ass mark on your neck. Now, with your reputation, who would he believe . . . me or you?" His phone stopped ringing. "I ain't leavin' here until I get what I came for." Zeke sat down on the love seat and stared at Red. He coughed a couple more times.

He's right, Red thought. *Q wouldn't believe me. He'd take this nigga's word over mine and I'd be back at square one. Think, Red, think!* "You know what," she proclaimed, "I ain't got time for this bullshit." She walked out of the living room and into her bedroom. Her head was pounding and she needed to get something to stop the migraine that was forming.

Opening the medicine cabinet, she located some Tylenol for migraines, but her eyes quickly diverted to the small clear bottle next to the package.

Red smiled, uncapped it and put it inside her waistband. She then opened the bottle of Tylenol, took two out, and placed the package back into the cabinet. Walking out of the bedroom, she passed Zeke again.

"You got it?" Zeke asked. He began to make funny throaty noises, like he was trying to suppress a cough, but couldn't.

She walked into the kitchen and retrieved two bottles of water out of the fridge. She opened hers and took the Tylenol. Once she returned to the living room, she handed Zeke a bottle. "You may need this." She heard him cough a few more times.

Zeke opened the bottle and began to drink. He immediately put it down as the water went down the wrong way. Red rushed to him and sat on the arm of the love seat as she started to pat his back. As she did that, she took her right hand, retrieved the small bottle from her pants and squeezed all of the clear liquid into the water. Once his coughing attack began to subside, she handed him his water again and he drank the rest of it. Red smiled as she saw the liquid disappear from the bottle and down his throat.

"Let me get my checkbook," Red said.

"Checkbook? Bitch, do I look like a bank? I gave you cash, I want cash in return."

"Okay. Damn, Zeke!"

"Naw, as a matter of fact, fuck it." He picked up his phone. "You stallin'." He began to punch in numbers.

"Who the fuck you callin'?"

"Q."

"Wait, Zeke," she said in a panicked tone. "Stop. You're right, I was stallin'."

Zeke began to breathe heavily, and Red's anxiety began to subside. *It's working.* "I was stalling because I can't let you fuck up what I have."

Zeke was now in distress. He couldn't breathe and his body was starting to convulse. Red watched on calmly. He reached out toward her as if she were his lifeline.

"You should have left well enough alone, Zeke, but this is what you get when you threaten me." She grabbed the two water bottles and their caps, made sure she had the empty Visine bottle and shoved everything in her purse. Zeke struggled to say "help me" during his gasps for breath, but Red walked out and left without bothering to close the door.

*R*ed drove away from the building in the Lincoln Navigator she'd rented upon her return to the States, hoping that Q did not return home anytime soon. Her adrenaline pumped high. She wanted Zeke to be dead or damn near dead before anyone found him. Driving for a few minutes Red began to come to her senses. She pulled over on the side of the street because her heart began racing.

"Should I go back?" she said out loud. She answered her own question: "No, Red, he was going to blackmail you. Why do people want me to act this way?" She began crying. "I'm trying to change, I'm trying!" She screamed out loud, put her hands up to her face and cried profusely.

After minutes of tearful torrents, Red reached into her side console and pulled out a travel pack of Kleenex. Pulling down her sun visor and looking into the mirror, she dabbed her eyes and blew her nose. Her eyes went to the big red mark that was starting to show on her neck. "That son of a bitch!" She held her head up, exposing the left side of her neck to get a good look at it, and then sighed. "Damn, Zeke! I didn't wanna hurt you, but I can't lose Q . . . for you or anyone."

Red gathered her composure, focused on the present and what she needed to do. The first course of action was to find Gloria. Once she got the check situation straightened out, she and Q could just leave. Start a new life somewhere else. "Yep, that's the answer. Find Gloria." She looked one more time in the mirror before flipping the visor back up. Red saw the faint mark of the cut on her nose, courtesy of Bacon. The deep wound of humiliation wouldn't heal until Red did something about it.

Over the last couple of days, she had been inquiring about Bacon but nobody had seen him or heard from him. Red wasn't sure of his whereabouts but she had to know.

Red arrived at Schottenstein Realty, hoping to catch Gloria. She noticed a lockbox on the front door. Perplexed, she pulled out her cell phone and dialed Gloria's number. The blare of a recording reported, "The cellular number you have called is no longer in service. Please check the number and dial again. Message 3492."

Red redialed and received the same message. Her heart started racing. What was going on? She thought back to the last time she saw Gloria—

"Oh, my God! The closing! Lord, please—"

She climbed into her car and sped off to the title company. All sorts of thoughts rushed through Red's mind. *Please don't let Gloria be in jail for some of my fraudulent real estate deals.* Red thought back to the closing, then back to the check. Gloria had vouched for her like a soldier, but Red would die if she was locked up all because of her. "My relationship with Q will be as good as over if I don't get this shit settled," Red said out loud.

• • •

"Good morning, Ms. Gomez," the cheerful blonde receptionist chirped.

"Good morning, Heather," Red read off her name badge. "Is Mr. Perch in?"

"Please, have a seat. I'll let him know you're here."

"Thank you." Red walked away from the reception desk to the water cooler. She put the small Styrofoam cup under the spout and pushed the blue button to dispense cold water.

"Ms. Gomez, he will see you now," the receptionist spoke just as Red put the cup up to her lips.

Red tossed the full cup into the trash as she made her way back to Mr. Perch's office.

"Good morning, Kevin," Red spoke.

"Raven," he acknowledged. "You're looking quite spectacu-lar." He pointed toward the seat in front of his desk. "What can I do for you today?"

"My commission check for the sale of thirty-one-twenty-four Colonnade Drive. I've tried to deposit it, but—"

"Right . . . right," Mr. Perch said, cutting her off. "Unfortu-nately, the sale of the property has been reviewed by an attorney and the sale isn't valid."

"What do you mean, not valid?"

"We were forced to put a stop payment on your commission check. Apparently when the documents were reviewed by the closing office, they were found to be incomplete."

"Excuse me? I've been doing this for two years, what do you mean incomplete?"

"Something about the identification of the sellers. They had your identification and signature. However, they had no identifi-cation for the other owner, only a signature. They need that person's photo ID."

"What?—This is . . . Where's Gloria?" Red demanded.

The man paused for a moment and looked at her.

"Where is Gloria? You so paper perfect but you deaf!" Red quickly jumped up and an angry scowl plastered her face.

Mr. Perch flinched. He hadn't expected this reaction from her. "Raven, I'm sorry to tell you this, but Gloria died a couple of weeks ago. Breast cancer."

Red stared at him. Mouthing the words "she died," Red fell back into the chair and tears suddenly began to flood her eyes. The next thing she knew she broke down and wept uncontrollably. Gloria had meant so much to her. She was the one person in her life who had believed in her. Gloria was like the mother she'd never had.

Mr. Perch gave Red the chance to gain composure on her own. He knew he couldn't console her; after all, she and Gloria were tight. Moments later, he spoke up. "I know it's hard to believe she's gone. We all miss her . . . Anyhow, she left something for you." He opened the drawer and handed Red a large white envelope. She opened it: there was a letter addressed to her, along with other material. She pulled out the letter and read it.

My Dearest Raven,

If you're reading this letter, it means I've gone on to a better place. My heart was broken when my husband died, and then you came along. You gave me reason for living and were the daughter I never had. You and I were a great team, but I still had that void. True love never dies.

Raven, don't cry for me. Live for me. I'm at peace and with my husband.

As promised, here are the keys to the office and lockbox. The business is yours, if you want it. Just sign the paperwork and make me proud.

I love you,
Gloria

Red looked in the envelope; all of the papers were in order for the transfer of the business, along with the keys, as well as her broker information. Red dried her tears and presented the contract to Mr. Perch.

"Well, Raven, looks like you have expensive shoes to fill." He smiled at her. Gloria wore nothing but the best and she expected the best.

"I'm speechless," Red confessed. "She meant so much to me." Tears began to fill her eyes again.

"And you meant a lot to her." He handed her a pen and Red began signing the papers for her new business. After she signed the last page, he watched as she got up and walked toward the door. "Raven?"

She turned around to address Mr. Perch. "Yes?"

"This is what Gloria wanted. I know you won't let her down."

"Thank you." Still feeling dazed, Red walked out of the door.

As she left the title company and drove to Schottenstein Realty, thoughts of Gloria flooded her mind. Once Red arrived, she used her keys to unlock the lockbox. She trudged into the quiet establishment and remembered what it was like. Gloria didn't have a lot of agents, but it was a close-knit family. Red didn't mingle much with her counterparts, but she and Gloria had their own special bond. Gloria believed in success at any level. Red remembered Gloria's motto: "Your reputation is all that you have in life, and all that you need in this industry." That translated easily into real life. Reputation and perception go hand in hand.

As if drawn on an invisible string, Red walked into Gloria's office and saw that nothing had been touched. All of her pictures, licenses and awards were on the wall. She sat down behind the desk and picked up a picture of Gloria and her husband, Sherman. *True love never dies*; she remembered the letter, and Gloria's words. Fingering the couple's photograph, Red could see how happy they had been together. All of a sudden, she wondered if she could ever be that happy—or would love always elude her because of her sordid past? Could she and Q get through all the lies and tricks she'd played on him? The fake pregnancy; the real one and not knowing who the father was; tricking him into buying the loft . . . it just seemed so minor to her.

But the check. He's gonna think I'm playing some type of game because I can't cash the check. Shit!

Q's curiosity got the best of him. His mother told him that she'd seen his ex-girlfriend, Chass, and gave him the business card she had given her. Since she didn't like Red's shady behavior, his mother didn't see anything wrong with trying to open her son's eyes.

Remembering Chass brought a barrage of emotions to Q's heart. They were together all through high school but their destinies were different. College called her; the streets called his name, loud and clear, introducing him to another world and a different caliber of women. Even though Chass was pretty enough, Q had access to nothing less than dime pieces and then along came along Red.

Q felt bad about how he left things with Chass, because she was with him when he had nothing, but from the looks of it, she'd made something of herself. She was now an attorney.

Should I or shouldn't I? Q wrestled with his emotions after looking at the card for several minutes. *She can either talk to me or hang up.*

He dialed the number and waited for someone to answer.

"Public Defenders' office, how may I help you?"

"Chass Reed, please."

"May I tell her who's calling?"

"Uh . . . tell her it's Quentin Carter."

After about fifteen seconds, he thought, *I can't do this to Red*. Just as he was about to hang up, a sweet-sounding voice on the other end answered.

"Quentin?"

"Hi . . . um . . . yes, it's me." His playa status was shot to shit. She caught him off guard.

This was an awkward time for Q. Chass wasn't just a notch on his belt. He truly cared for her at one time.

"I was hoping your mother would give you my card."

"Yeah . . . yeah, she did." Silence. "Well hey, it looks like you doin' good for yourself. You a big-time attorney now, huh?"

"Not big-time yet," she laughed. "I got out of law school not too long ago." An awkward silence filled the air. "I'm working on a case here, then afterward, I'm going home."

"Home? Where's home?"

"New York." More silence. "How's Zeke, Quentin?" Chass knew many of Q's friends, especially Zeke.

"He ain't change much, still the same crazy-ass Zeke." They both laughed.

More silence.

"Quentin, I gotta go but I'd like to see you before my case is over."

He thought about it for a moment. "I'd like that," he said. He hung up the phone after exchanging numbers. On his way back to the loft he called Zeke and left a message. "Yo, you'd never believe who I just got off the phone with! Hit me back!"

Red sat in Gloria's office torn up over what she had done to Zeke. Having committed a treacherous act against Q her emotions played tricks on her. *Would he be better off dead or alive? Shit, I'm not the one who decided that,* she convinced herself. *He did. It was his choice. At least if he's dead, he can't talk, but if he's alive, then . . .* Red shook the thought out of her mind.

She'd already called a sign maker to put up the name of the new ownership—Gomez Realty. She was determined to carry on where Gloria left off. Unfortunately, she would have to watch her spending until she made more money. The $1.6 million check was no good, and she only had a little over $200,000 in the bank. For someone like Red, that could be gone in a heartbeat. Red thought back to what was said at the title company.

"Unfortunately, the sale of the property has been reviewed by an attorney and the sale isn't valid."

"What do you mean, not valid?"

"We were forced to put a stop payment on your commission check."

But what's up with the property? she thought. *If the transaction is null and void, that means the property is still in my name . . . and Bacon's.*

CHAPTER 18

*I*t was Friday afternoon and Big Will's Barbershop was packed. The hum of clippers tightening up the latest styles could be heard while raucous laughter and jonin' filled the air as two young cats battled in *Smackdown vs. Raw* on the PlayStation 3. Some enjoyed the videos on *106 & Park* on the wall-mounted plasma TV while others were tuned into a DVD of Farrakhan delivering one of his powerful speeches.

Q sauntered in after deciding not to go home right away and was greeted by many of the patrons.

"What's up, my brotha?" Big Will acknowledged, then picked up another set of clippers and began to tighten up Mekel's taper.

"What's up?" Q said as the two men exchanged a dap. "How many ahead of me?" Q looked around at the men in the shop.

"Just Mekel here." Big Will knew and called each of his customers by name. He felt that doing so would promote brotherhood and unity among black men in the community.

Q sat down and waited his turn while engaging in light conversation with Mekel. They'd met at the hospital when Kera gave birth, and again at Red's, but they knew more of each other through word of mouth on the streets. They respected each other's hustles.

Little did they know, they had a lot in common. They both had loved ones who went down because of the game, and the book *Bitch Nigga, Snitch Nigga* told it all. They were both determined to avenge their loved ones' untimely demises. And they also knew their women were partnas at one point.

"How's the baby, man?" Q asked Mekel.

"He's doing good, real good," Mekel said, with a proud beam on his face.

"So you settlin' down, huh? Gonna be that one-woman man," Q teased. Big Will removed the cape from around Mekel's neck.

"Man," Mekel said, standing up, "that was good then, but it's hard to stay with one woman." He reached into his pocket, then paid Big Will.

"I feel ya," another man chimed in. "A nigga shouldn't just have one woman when pussy is plentiful!" Everyone erupted in laughter.

"Shit, I made my money off women," Mekel said truthfully. "I ain't used to this. At first I thought she was going through that postpartum stuff, but now she's at church all the time, sprinkling holy oil, holy water, whatever that shit is all around the house, mood swings all over the place . . . I don't know what's up with her."

"Aww shit!" a young dude commented. "The church done got ahold of her now. Next she gon' be talking about that premarital sex stuff. She like a hawk now, flyin' in a circle. She gon' get yo' ass. You better run while you got the chance!"

More laughter erupted. Mekel had to laugh at that himself because he could envision Kera snappin' on him, or better yet, tying him to a chair and throwing holy water on him.

Q sat down in the chair and Big Will draped the cape around his neck. Q and Mekel engaged in conversation for a moment. Then right before Mekel left the shop, the two promised to stay in touch with each other.

As Mekel was entering his truck, his cell phone rang. The caller ID read Unavailable, but he answered it anyway.

"Yeah." He started the truck and immediately was engulfed in music.

The automated message stated he had a collect call from an inmate at a correctional center, but the caller's name was inaudible due to his loud music. He pressed five.

"Mekel?"

"Who dis?" he said, trying to sound hard.

"This is Terry, but before you hang up," she said in a torrent of words, "please hear me out."

"You got twenty seconds," Mekel barked angrily as he began to drive.

"I called you the other day at home and Kera answered and wouldn't let me talk to you. But that's not the reason I'm calling. I'm calling because I'm going to court in two days and I wanted you to know that I was wrong for my actions and I accept full responsibility for whatever the outcome is. Just know I didn't do it to hurt the baby. I would never do that. I was hurt because I loved you and you didn't love me back."

Mekel's cell beeped, alerting him that he had another call. He looked at the caller ID and paused.

"Mekel?" Terry called out, thinking he hung up on her.

"I'm here."

There was an uncomfortable silence. Then she continued. "Well . . . my time is up. I'm gonna go now."

"No, Terry, wait."

Another long silence, with Terry waiting to hear what he had to say.

Finally Mekel spoke up. "I will never forgive you for what you did, but I will always care for you and I'm sorry for how things turned out." He stopped talking and swallowed hard. The person trying to get through hung up. "How are they treating you in there?"

"They got me undergoing a lot of psychological testing, but I lost my kids. Mama flipped the script and said I was never home because I was chasing you."

"Damn, that's rough."

"Yeah, but it's okay though. At least they're not in the system, and I know they're being taken care of. Hopefully I'll be home soon and I'll be able to be their mother again."

"Regardless of who raises them, Terry, you will always be their mother."

"Thanks, Mekel. I needed to hear that."

Mekel drove the rest of the way home talking to her.

CHAPTER 19

Red looked at the clock on the wall. Four P.M. She had been at the office a couple of hours. There was a serenity in the air that she needed after the violent act she'd committed earlier. Red's emotions went from hot to cold. She was like a black panther—back her up in a corner, she'd come out clawing, not caring who would be hurt in the process. She thought back to her unborn child and how it was taken away from her at the hands of another person. *Did my child deserve to die? No! Does Zeke deserve to die?* she challenged herself. *He's just as much a person as my baby was.* Red thought about it, battling her conscience. But her self-absorption won out. *Hell, yeah,* she thought, *that nigga deserves whatever he got comin' to him. He could jeopardize my relationship with Q. I don't know who he thought he was fuckin' with, but I'd put a stop to anyone who dares to stand in the way!*

Her mind flashed to Bacon. "Let me see something," she said out loud, firing up her Apple laptop computer. Over the last few days, she had been hearing Bacon's name on the streets but nobody had seen him. She had to see for herself if he was truly out. She typed in www.bop.gov, then entered his required information and waited for the results to display.

"Gotdamnit!" she said out loud. There was a date by his name, as well as the word RELEASED. So he wasn't out through an escape. Somehow he had beat his case. She shook her head, ruefully.

Red remembered the book and her thoughts went to Catfish. She pulled out a pen and paper and began to write:

> *Catfish,*
>   *We need to talk. Please put me on your visitor list so I can come see you. I want to squash some things before they get out of hand.*
>
> *Red*

Red addressed the envelope with the information she received from the website and decided to take it to the post office once she left.

Red thought of Q and what her life would be like with him out of the game. She scowled. She then thought of the other people who had done her wrong . . . the ones who called themselves her friends. "I got something for Kera sending that damned letter to Bacon. Terry's dumb ass still owe me money, and Sasha?" Red shook her head thinking of Sasha and Blue together. "You crossed the ultimate line." The thought of the three women and what they had done to her angered Red even more.

She looked to her right and saw Gloria's Rolodex of clients. She remembered how Gloria started in the business. *I built my company with one client. That client later referred me to another client, then another.*

Red had truly learned a legal hustle, but she needed something to jump-start her new venture. Finally, she came up with an idea. She decided to host an open house.

Feeling better about everything, Red began to map out her plans. She had tons to do and very little time to do it.

Red made plans to contact an advertising agency to help with the introduction of Gomez Realty; she would also place ads in upscale magazines to gain her clientele. She knew the business; she just had to get out there and start working again.

One thing she'd learned while in Mexico was how to be happy with what you have now. Red had realized that although she didn't have what she was accustomed to at first—the fly clothes, the expensive car, the money and a man—she had to make it by the sweat of her brow. In her heart, she was truly ready to turn her life around to be with Q, but somehow she knew that all of her dirtiness wouldn't disappear.

A strange tone rang from her cell phone. She grabbed it and looked at the caller ID.

"Who in the fuck is calling me private?" Red hated that.

Though she wasn't one to answer her phone if the person wouldn't display their number, she answered it anyway.

"Hello? Hello?"

Nobody said anything.

Red hung up. Just then, she looked up and saw a car, a BMW that looked like her old car, the one Bacon bought her. Almost instantly, her cell rang again. "Damn, who is it this time?" She looked at the caller ID and saw unknown.

"What!" she yelled into the phone.

To her surprise, it turned out to be a collect call from Terry. Tempted to hang up, she decided to fuck with Terry, so she pushed five and accepted the call.

"Bitch, you got some clothes for me?" Terry quipped, in hopes Red wouldn't go off on her after she heard her voice.

"I ain't got nothing that goes with county colors," Red replied coldly.

"Damn, Red, can you at least be civil to a bitch?"

"What do you want, Terry? I'm in the middle of something."

"I was just calling, you know." Terry realized it was a mistake to call Red, but she continued. She hoped their longtime friendship would mean something to Red. "Since I been in here, I had a lot of time to think and I've learned something about myself." Terry was excited about the breakthrough she had made and wanted to share it with someone, even if it was with Red.

"And I suppose you're gonna tell me what it is, huh?" Red asked sarcastically.

Ignoring Red's attitude, Terry spoke. "I learned that I am responsible for my own actions. Nobody controls what I do, except me."

"Umpf," Red grunted. "You know that was fucked up what you did, right?"

"Yeah, I know," Terry confirmed. "The baby didn't—"

"Baby? I ain't talking 'bout no damn baby," Red yelled. "That *was* fucked up, but I'm talking about you acting like you was in the Wild Wild West at my gotdamn house. You still owe me for that shit."

"Red, you still stuck on that?" Terry spat.

"Yeah, you still owe me. What was the deal, two thousand and your truck?"

Terry couldn't believe her ears. She was behind bars until God only knew when and all Red could think about was her house.

"You know what, Red . . . I don't know why the hell I called you. You only care about yourself."

"You ain't know?" Red replied coldly. "Now, are we gonna work this out or should the authorities get a little tape in the mail? You wanna hear it, it's right here," Red lied.

"Ooh, Red, I can't stand you!" Terry remembered the tape

Red had with her confession that she'd shot at Mekel and Kera. "You'll never change. You still dirty."

"You're right," Red admitted, proudly.

Terry hung up.

If it weren't for Red not knowing what was up with her house, she would have gone there to get the tape. She loved fucking with Terry. Red smiled at her cell phone and turned it off.

"Oh, my God! Zeke!" Q yelled. He had just returned to the loft and found his friend lying on the floor with white foam spewing from his mouth. Q looked around the living room and noticed that picture frames were broken and lying on the floor. Immediately, he dialed 911.

"Operator, I need an ambulance! I found my friend passed out on the floor. He doesn't look too good."

"Is he breathing?" the operator asked.

"I don't know. Let me check." Q knelt over his boyhood friend and placed his finger under his nose. He felt faint but sporadic air coming from his nostrils. "Yes! He's still breathing, barely."

"Hold on."

Within minutes, three paramedics came barreling through the door with a stretcher and large black medical bags. Seconds later, Zeke had an oxygen mask over his nose and mouth, and an IV coming out of his left arm. The three men lifted Zeke's motionless body onto the stretcher and whisked him to the ambulance.

Q tried to follow the paramedics, but was stopped by two law enforcement officers.

"Excuse me, Mr. Carter?"

"Yes," Q answered.

"We'd like to ask you a few questions about what happened here. I'm Officer McDonald, and my partner is Officer Thomas."

"Look, can we do this later? That's my boy and—"

"This will only take a minute," Office McDonald assured Q, cutting him off. Q noticed the skinny young black officer, Officer Thomas, looking around the loft. Q eyed him cautiously.

"Can you tell me what happened?"

"I . . . I don't know," Q answered truthfully. "I just came home and he was here on the floor with stuff coming out of his mouth, barely breathing."

"What did you do when you found him?"

Q looked at him like he was crazy. "I called 911, what . . ." He threw his hands up in the air and twisted his mouth in disgust.

"I'm sorry, Mr. Carter," Officer McDonald said. "These are just standard questions. Where were you?"

"Where was I when?" Q snapped. "I was here when I called."

"No. Where were you while Ezekiel Morrison was in your home?"

"I had some runs to make."

"Some runs?"

"Yeah . . . look, man, I don't have time for this. My doorman saw me leave, and he saw me when I came back." The two looked at each other as if in a Mexican standoff.

Officer Thomas saw the tension and walked over to them. "There's nothing here," he told his partner. "Mr. Carter, if we need anything else, we'll be in touch. Sorry for any inconvenience."

The officers left and Q followed right behind them, heading to Scott Memorial Hospital. En route, he called Red's cell phone, but her voice mail picked up immediately. He left a message telling her he was going to the hospital. Q needed to talk to someone and he knew just who to call. He drove feverishly to get to the hospital, all the while praying that his boy wouldn't die.

Chass greeted Q at the entrance and they made their way to the Emergency waiting area. Q was glad she was there for him, and she was glad that Q called her. Chass comforted him while they waited for Zeke's prognosis.

Blue looked over at Sasha as she slept. He didn't want to wake her because she had put in a lot of work over the last few days. While he was in New York handling business, she was traveling from Jersey to Pennsylvania, making sure his money was right. With her, it was like having Blue in two places at the same time; however, nobody would suspect Sasha to be his eyes and ears. Her knowledge of the drug game and her loyalty to him was more than he had expected.

Just hours ago, he was trying to kill her with his dick; she held her own and with every stroke he gave, her pussy challenged him to continue to bring it on.

Before that, Blue had been waiting for Sasha to return from New Jersey—she was running late. All sorts of thoughts flooded his mind. *Did she get popped? Nah . . . I would have heard about that. Damn, I know she don't call herself taking my shit and runnin' with it.*

About thirty minutes later, Sasha walked through the door.

"Where the fuck you been?" Blue yelled at her.

"Damn, nigga, chill!" Sasha had to pee. She slid the large black purse that was on her shoulder to the floor, held her crotch and trotted off to the bathroom. She almost peed on herself before her bottom hit the toilet seat. After finishing her business, she washed her hands, then went back in the hallway to deal with Blue. "Now, what the hell is your problem?"

"You're late. Where's my shit?" he barked.

"You know what?" Sasha said, walking over to the bag she dropped. "I'm tired of you acting like I'ma do something with yo' stuff. Here, boy!" She reached in and threw four large bundles of money at him. One hitting him upside the head.

"Boy?"

"Yeah, *BOY!* That's what you actin' like . . . like someone gon' take yo' shit. When are you gonna realize I got yo' back?" Sasha now had tears in her eyes. She felt like no matter how hard she tried to show him she was true, Blue always did something to fuck it up. Blue knew she was down for him, but he just couldn't trust a female. Sasha was no exception, or so he thought.

"Damn, ma, don't cry on me and shit," he said when he saw a tear fall from her eyes onto her beautiful dark brown skin. "I hate when you do that." Blue walked up to her and wiped away her tears. "You know, it's just hard for me, in my line of work, to be able to trust someone, ya know."

Sasha turned to walk away, but Blue grabbed her arm. "What the fuck you want now?" She was pissed at him.

Blue backed her up forcefully against the wall. He began kissing her roughly. Sasha reciprocated not only with kisses, but small bites. Blue roughly put his hands under her blouse and ripped it off of her. Sasha couldn't wait for his hands to touch her breasts. She reached back and unhooked her bra, letting her breasts free. Blue grabbed them forcefully and began sucking on one, then the other.

"Ooh . . . shh . . . ooh, that feels good," she panted. Her breasts were tender but his hot mouth on the nipples made every nerve ending in her body stand up.

Blue tugged at Sasha's pants. She eased her way out of them. She stood before him in only her panties. He picked her up and carried her to the bedroom. He needed some type of leverage with what he was going to do to her. She bounced once when he tossed her on the bed. Quickly undressing, Blue hopped on the bed and with his right hand moved her left leg as far as it could go, and entered her forcefully. One stroke . . . two stokes . . . "Damn, ma, this shit . . ." he grunted as he tried to knock her back out.

The two fucked like wild animals, clawing, biting, pulling at each other. The heightened sensations made them climax repeatedly.

Although Blue had schooled Red, Sasha schooled him that seasoned pussy didn't have to be trained. And she was right. Once more, she had proven herself, and Blue was definitely feeling her.

Looking at Sasha sleep soundly, he remembered the reason why he hooked up with her in the first place. Even though she called him, he had been trying to find a way to get back to her. There was a nice bounty on her head. At first he thought it would be simple, but now he realized the money he was offered to bring her back to Catfish, dead or alive, meant nothing. He had to protect her, and that he would do, at all costs.

The sound of the running water from the shower awakened Sasha. She surprised him with her presence as she eased into the shower to share with him, but it would have to wait till later. She knew they were headed back to Detroit. He had a new connect and a new product, Black Tar, and it was selling like crazy, but they wouldn't be leaving until she got hers, again.

$\mathcal{B}$aby," Mekel called out when he entered the apartment. "You home?" There was no answer. Enjoying the peace for however long he could, he stripped down to his boxers and stretched out on the bed. He thought about Terry and everything that was revealed during their conversation. Then he began to daydream about the last time they had sex.

Mekel stepped out of the shower and Terry stood there with her ass exposed. He rejected her advances at first, but he hadn't gotten his nut off in several weeks, so the blood left his brain and went to his other head. He watched in the mirror as she deep-throated him. Terry was a pro with her head game. He nutted in her mouth, then pulled out slightly and continued nutting on the side of her face. He then ripped Terry's shirt from her body, bent her over the sink and proceeded to bang her back out, looking for nut number two.

The memory was all too real.

Three hours later, Mekel awakened, fully rested. He looked down at his sheets and saw the mess he had made. He'd jacked off again to his memory of his and Terry's last encounter. He'd been doing that a lot lately. Immediately, he began to snatch the sheets off. Just as he threw the sheets into the washing machine and started the suds to sloshing about, he heard the front door slam. He rushed into the living room, feeling guilty for pleasuring himself at the thought of Terry in the bed that he and Kera shared. It was Kera, but she didn't have the baby with her.

"Hey, baby," he said, cheerfully. He noticed she looked disheveled. "Where's the baby?"

"In the hospital."

"The hospital?"

"Yeah. The babysitter called and said he was unresponsive when she tried to wake him up from his nap. When she picked him up, he started shaking really bad."

"What?!" Mekel yelled.

"Mekel, they say he has some type of seizure disorder," Kera admitted through tears. "I tried to call you earlier from the Emergency Room, but you didn't answer your phone."

Mekel cringed, remembering the calls that he'd ignored when he was talking to Terry earlier. He began to pace the floor. "Man!" Suddenly, he rushed to the bedroom and began to put his clothes on. Kera followed him. "What . . ." She paused, looking at the stripped bed. "What happened here, Mekel?" He continued to put his clothes on. "Did you have another woman over?" Mekel looked at her like she lost her mind.

"Where are you going?"

"To the hospital to see my son."

"What about me, Mekel?"

"He's a baby, Kera. He needs his parents. Come on."

"You didn't think about that when I was calling you earlier. He only had his mother then," Kera spat. "You know what? This is all your fault."

Transfixed with shock, Mekel stared at Kera as though seeing her for the first time. "*My* fault?"

"Yeah, yours. If you would have been man enough to handle your business when I first told you I was pregnant, none of this would have happened."

"Kera, don't start. This ain't the time," Mekel warned as he began to step into his Tims.

"Terry would have had enough time to get used to y'all being broken up. So because of you"—Kera poked her finger in his chest—"she reacted, and now my child has this . . . this . . . thing!"

Mekel, sick of the constant barbs, grabbed a cap and his keys and headed toward the front door.

"Where are you going?" she yelled behind him.

"Out!" Mekel slammed the door, causing it to leap on its hinges, and left Kera in the apartment in tears.

Mekel drove around for what seemed like hours. He ended up at Scott Memorial. His heart ached at the thought of his son not being perfectly healthy. *This is all your fault,* he remembered Kera saying to him. With a tear in his eye as he exited his truck, he thought, *she's right. If I had stopped the shit before it got outta hand, none of us would be in this situation.*

Jogging through the sliding glass doors of the hospital, he received directions to his son's location in the pediatric neurology unit from the information desk. The elevator ride to the sixth floor was the longest ride he had ever taken. As the elevator chimed, to alert him he was on his desired floor, he heaved a deep breath and scurried out in search for his son. Following the directions for the room number, he finally arrived, and found the door partially opened. He heard voices, and hesitated for a moment before walking in.

He found several medical personnel examining lil' Mekel.

"Wh . . . what's happening?" he asked.

"Mr. Chambers, I presume?" the doctor asked. Mekel nodded. "Your son had a miniseizure earlier, but he's stabilized. He sure is a trouper." Mekel smiled at that assessment. "At any rate, we've called in the pediatric neurology specialists from Johns Hopkins. They should be here in a couple of days."

"Thank you," Mekel responded as he stepped closer to the crib and looked at his namesake. "Can you explain why this happened?"

The doctor cast Mekel a strange look.

Mekel wondered why the doctor was looking at him in such a puzzled manner. He gave the nurse some orders and led Mekel to another room.

"Mr. Chambers, do you know why your son was brought into the Emergency Room today?"

"I was told he was unresponsive and started shaking really bad."

"Is that all?"

"Look, what's wrong with my son? Tell me what happened and how we can fix this."

"Mr. Chambers, your son has fetal alcohol syndrome," the doctor explained.

"Fetal who?" Mekel repeated blankly.

"Fetal alcohol syndrome. Early in your wife's pregnancy, she exposed the unborn child to large amounts of alcohol and narcotics."

"*Narcotics?*" Mekel yelled. He had never known Kera to do any type of drugs. The drinking was a definite possibility because oftentimes they drank before they got buck. "Kera doesn't—"

"Mr. Chambers," the doctor interrupted, "you can take that up with your wife later, but the concern now is with your son.

Mrs. Chambers mentioned that you are the primary caregiver of your son. Is that true?"

"Yes." Mekel tried to be proud of this fact but he didn't think the doctor thought otherwise.

"Didn't you see anything that would make you question your son's development?"

Flashbacks flooded Mekel's mind—the look in the swing, the inability to hold his head up without support, the constant cries when he was not held tightly . . . Mekel didn't equate these things to a specific problem. He thought it was typical behavior for babies. He was a proud father, and was just glad to have his son around.

Now Mekel was furious. Fetal alcohol syndrome was totally preventable. It was senseless abuse of an unborn child and he was surprised that Kera, who he thought was proud of her pregnancy from the beginning, would have done something so stupid.

"So, Doctor," Mekel said, hesitantly, "are seizures common with this fetal alcohol syndrome, or could they have been caused by something else?"

"Something else like what?"

"Like being dropped."

"Dropped? When was he dropped?" The doctor pulled out a pad and began taking notes.

Mekel sighed. Kera obviously hadn't told him of the incident. After Mekel explained everything, the doctor finished his note-taking, closed the pad and spoke.

"Well, Mr. Chambers, at this stage, the fall would have only aggravated the condition, but this would have happened regardless. I'm sorry to say your son won't be 'normal' in the clinical sense, but with help, training and support groups, you and your wife will be able to raise him in a normal environment." The doctor stopped; he was being paged. "I have to go, but you may go see your son. He's a sweet child."

Mekel followed the doctor out and walked back to lil' Mekel's hospital room.

She knew, he said to himself. *Wife? Why does he keep referring to Kera as my wife? Damn, I wonder what else she's telling them, but not telling me.* He walked over to the crib. It looked like a big cage.

"Would you like to hold your son?" the nurse asked as she changed the IV bag.

"Yes," Mekel answered, and sat in the oversize rocker next to the crib.

The nurse showed him how push the button and to call for help if he needed it as she placed the baby in his arms, then left.

Mekel looked down at his son who was now wide awake. His son looked up at him with his big doe eyes, and smiled.

"Everything will be okay, lil' man. Daddy's here."

"I know this nigga ain't," Foxy yelled and slammed the phone down, "trying to avoid me!" She hadn't heard from him since he left that night he tried to kill Q and Red. She didn't want to admit it but she had actually started to care for him because he fucked her so well. "This nigga better be somewhere near death," she said as she sucked her teeth. "He don't get none of this and just bounce."

Nightfall came and Bacon sat outside of Foxy's apartment. She had been calling him for some time now, but he couldn't bring himself to go back over there until now. He was angry that she could have possibly been fucking Q too, but tonight he needed to get up in some pussy. The stuck-up hos that Maurice had running through the crib reminded him too much of Red. Gold diggers. He needed some appreciative pussy.

Bacon walked up to Foxy's door and tapped.

No answer.

He tapped again.

"Who is it?" a groggy female voice answered. He didn't speak, just tapped again.

This time, Foxy flung the door open, but the first thing Bacon saw was the baseball bat. He smiled.

"What do you want?" Foxy snapped.

"You gonna keep a brotha waiting out here?" Bacon said.

"I ain't got time for no games," Foxy confirmed. "Now I don't know who the fuck you are, so you best step off."

Bacon couldn't believe Foxy didn't recognize him. "I got something you know very well," he said, toying with her.

Disgusted, Foxy attempted to close the door, but Bacon stopped her. "Foxy, it's me, Bacon." He had to play his hand because he wanted to fuck and if Foxy closed the door on him, that would be it.

She looked at him closely. "What . . . I can't . . ." She saw the truth, then snapped, "You know what, fuck you, muthafucka! I ain't heard from you since when?"

Bacon attempted to calm her down, then followed her in the house. It wasn't long before Foxy realized it was truly indeed Bacon. He didn't waste any time getting up in her. Foxy played hard to get as long as she could, but she needed him.

Afterward, Foxy lay on Bacon's chest and stroked her sweat-drenched weave. "Anyone been up in my shit since I been gone?" he asked.

"Yo' shit? Hah! Last I remembered, this belonged to Ms. Foxy. You just a guest up in it."

Bacon laughed. He knew he couldn't claim anything, especially when he wasn't considering Foxy for wifey.

"What you know good?" he inquired.

"Did you think about what I said last time?" Foxy asked, ignoring his question.

"What?"

"Pursuing the second book deal."

Bacon began stroking his cum-drained dick. "Yeah, actually, I *got* a second book deal, but I need a favor from you."

Bacon's erection prevented him from telling Foxy what he needed her to do because he wanted to fuck again.

Hours later, Bacon sat on the side of the bed, trying to get up.

"You heard from Red?" Foxy asked.

"Nah, I ain't fuckin' with that bitch."

"I heard that ho started her own real estate business and she's gonna have an open house soon. Word has it, she doesn't have a lot of money, so she may list your house again."

"What about that nigga Q?" Bacon inquired.

"He's keepin' time with someone else, but I know he still with Red. I think this woman and him have some type of history."

"What about you and Q?"

"Me and Q?" Foxy sucked her teeth. "Nothin'. We go way back. We just friends. Don't worry, baby, this is all yours."

Before Bacon left for the night, Foxy agreed to do what he asked.

CHAPTER 21

Q, Q baby!"

A frantic voice echoed through the Emergency Room halls. Red had checked her voice mail after leaving the post office, then headed straight to the hospital. She gave a sigh of relief when she spotted Q. "What's wrong?" She grabbed his hands and started inspecting him as if he had been in an accident.

"It's not me, it's—"

"Quentin," Chass interrupted, walking up to him. She nodded toward the doctor. Red looked at the woman who stood before her leading her man away. *Who the fuck is this ho? I know this nigga ain't playing me to the left for that homely looking bitch.* Red wanted to snatch what she thought was a weave off the woman's head, but she listened to what the doctor had to say. *I'll deal with this bitch in a minute.*

"Mr. Carter," an ER doctor called out. Q's heart began to pound at record speed with each step he took toward the man.

"How's my friend?"

"I'm sorry, Mr. Carter. We did all we could."

Q dropped his head in despair. "You're trying to tell me that Zeke is . . . dead?!" he yelled loudly.

Red attempted to hide her satisfied smirk.

"Again, I'm sorry. We have to notify his family for—"

"I am his family!" Q spat angrily.

"Quentin, come on," Chass told him softly.

"Aw no, heifer. You ain't taking him anywhere," Red barked. "I can take care of my man—find your own!" She stalked up to Chass, pointing her finger in the other woman's face.

"Red, stop! This ain't the time or place for your bullshit!" Q bellowed and walked away.

Chass followed him, leaving Red standing in the middle of the ER floor. This was the first time she'd seen the woman who took Q away from her and deep down, Chass was satisfied with Q's reaction.

In a huff, Red left the hospital. She had bigger fish to fry and she'd deal with Q at home. *One down, how many more to go?* she thought as she got back into the Navigator.

A few hours later lil' Mekel was sleeping peacefully, so Mekel went down to the main level to get some air. As soon as he walked outside, he saw someone who looked familiar, pacing back and forth.

"Hey, man, wha'sup?" Mekel questioned.

Q looked up. "They brought my boy in here earlier. He just died."

"Aw shit, I'm sorry," Mekel told him.

"Yeah, it's fucked up. What you doin' here?" Q asked.

"My son is in here," Mekel admitted.

"Damn, the baby?"

"Yeah. I can't believe this, man. He's just an innocent kid."

"Man, I'm sorry. If you need anything . . ."

"Thanks." They one-arm hugged again.

Just then, two wannabe thugs loped by with a dip and a bounce in their steps. Q noticed the taller of the two clutched a copy of *Bitch Nigga, Snitch Nigga* under his arm, and they were in deep discussion about it.

"Damn, this whore called out all these niggas!"

"Yeah, man, I tell ya. Let a bitch in on yo' bidness, they gon' fuck ya every time! That's why I don't let 'em talk. Every time dey ask a question, they get a dick in dey mouth."

They laughed, dapped and continued to stroll down the hospital's front sidewalk.

"I wonder what that shit's about?" Mekel asked.

Q looked at him like he was crazy. "Man, you ain't know?"

"What?"

"Remember the murder at Reason Why?" Mekel raised his eyebrows in curiosity. "The book out goes into detail about a drug deal gone bad, how it was all a setup and who ran their mouths," Q summarized.

"What's the name of the book?"

"*Bitch Nigga, Snitch Nigga*," Q told him.

"Where can I get a copy?" Mekel asked, seriously.

"You can check the gift shop here, but I doubt if they have it. It's really big now, though; even some of the Barnes and Nobles have it, but I got a copy in the car if you wanna read it," Q offered. He was glad to get his mind off of Zeke, even momentarily.

"My uncle went down over that shit." Mekel attempted to hide his anger, but was unsuccessful.

"Your uncle?"

"Yep, Larry Chambers." Mekel wasn't afraid to reveal the information because Larry was one of the top dope men on the streets and niggas couldn't touch him.

"Damn, it's a small world," Q admitted.

"Damn right, but what's really fucked up was that nigga Scooney got set up. My uncle said he'd never forget how that day went down. Scooney was his nigga—he was just at the wrong place at the wrong time. That nigga Catfish used to own the club and he was with that other nigga, Bacon. According to the book, and some other shit I know, Bacon, Catfish and his girl was up in the club and some shit kicked off. Scooney was shot on the dance floor while he was dancing with Catfish's woman. She helped set him up. The bitch was a decoy. Problem is that nigga had hos all over the place. Who knows who could have been with him then? This book is doing a lot of name-dropping and somebody gonna get hurt before it's over."

Q now remembered when he'd first read the passage in the book that alluded to Catfish.

> In the hood he was known as a stand-up nigga, but, in fact, he was a snitch bitch nigga. He had beady eyes that were unforgettable and resembled one of God's creatures. In the Bible, it said Jesus used this creature to feed a multitude of men. But in reality, there was no way God would use this creature, for it was the foulest in the land. It was a known scavenger. It would eat anything and live in the dirtiest conditions. It was even sacrilegious for Muslims to touch or eat. This Bitch Nigga, Snitch Nigga was named appropriately on the streets.

Although Q never told anyone about his affiliation with anyone in the book, Mekel knew because of his uncle, Larry, who was the head of the Chambers Brothers, who was now in prison. Q thought back to the acknowledgments in the book:

Shouts out to the Chamber-Brothers, Y.B.I.s, Best Friends Organization, East Side BK's, White Boy Rick, and the Earl Flynns. To all the Bitch Niggas, Snitch Niggas in these organizations, it is because of your mouths that we didn't survive.

Eyes were always looking, even from the grave and the cell, and as Q grew into a young man, little did he know, he was always protected.

On the many occasions that Mekel had visited Larry after Mekel's group, the Best Friends, disbanded, Larry commended him on being a more cautious hustler and encouraged him to go it alone. He had always mentioned Scooney's nephew, but all they called him was Q, and that was a common name on the streets.

Q dragged himself to his truck to get the book and returned. Mekel took it and said he'd get in touch with him once he finished reading the book.

Three weeks later, Kera sat in the chair while her stylist put the finishing touches on her simple ponytail.

Kera made the biggest decision of her life, when she completely dedicated her life to the Lord. She got rid of all of her trendy clothing and switched to a more subdued look, one that she claimed the Lord would be proud of—long skirts and blouses that didn't show much skin. She nixed the makeup and used Vaseline on her lips if needed. The only jewelry she wore was the dainty gold cross that Mekel bought her shortly after she gave birth. Kera was now truly low maintenance.

She spent all of her time either at work, church or home. Kera was determined not to let her family fall apart and prayed that the Lord would keep them together. She repented for her sins and wanted to talk to Mekel about forgiveness. She wanted to do it a while ago but was embarrassed that her foolish actions harmed their child. Mainly, though, she was not ready to face him. She'd said some harsh things that she knew she couldn't take back and hoped that with time, wounds would heal.

For weeks Kera prayed that God would give her a sign that Mekel wouldn't turn her away and today was the day. Every time she thought about talking to him, it rained, but today it didn't.

Kera had gained a lot of popularity because she'd had Mekel's baby. Not only was he fine, he was a well-known ladies' man. Although many girls had tried, not many succeeded. Terry was definitely a cock blocker when it came down to Mekel. But Kera happened to luck up. She was at the right place at the right time and ended up carrying Mekel's seed. But all that glittered wasn't gold.

Terry had fucked up when she bragged to everyone how well Mekel fucked her, and that curiosity had piqued Kera's interest. It wasn't just a coincidence she was in Vegas when he was. She wouldn't have known that he was in Vegas if Terry hadn't mentioned it. Kera knew he had other women, but that was before her, she'd surmised. Kera was vexed because Mekel wouldn't return her phone calls, or her text messages. Rapidly moving her fingers across the keyboard of her phone she typed, *I'm sorry. Call home, the baby needs us*, but got no response.

Kera was hurt that she hadn't heard from Mekel since he walked out three weeks ago but she kept constant tabs on him. Thanks to the nurses at the hospital, she learned of Mekel's comings and goings and made sure to never run into him while she visited their son.

But today, she was hoping she'd run into him because she missed him and what he had to offer. Before she met Mekel, she often did her thing with small-time niggas, but Mekel was the biggest catch yet, and she wasn't going to go back to what she used to be.

Mekel marched into the hospital room and took his place with his son. He wondered why the testing was taking so long. Every day he brought children's books to read to him, and a small radio to play music. The doctor had told him that reading to him and listening to music would stimulate his brain, possibly making his seizures less traumatic, but Mekel had more on his mind than just his son. He was thinking of Terry.

After her first phone call, he'd started visiting her once a week. He looked at his son and wondered what could have been if things were different. His mind drifted back to a conversation he had with Terry during his first visit.

Mekel walked into the visiting area and waited for Terry to emerge. He was shocked when he saw her. The makeup, jewelry and nails were gone. On top of it, she was forced to keep her hair in braids. She couldn't maintain her weave in prison.

A pregnant pause filled the air as she looked at him, face-to-face, for the first time since the attempted kidnapping. Terry sat down.

"Thanks for coming to see me, Mekel."

"Honestly, Terry, I don't know why I'm here."

Terry began to make small talk to break the tension between them. She spoke of the many women who were doing bids for their men. Many were there because of the drug trade but a handful weren't. Regardless of their crime, they were all there for the same reason. Their emotions guided them into doing something for a man, who more than likely wouldn't hold them down while they were sent up the river for them.

"Terry, tell me something," Mekel said.

"Sure."

"Tell me about your relationships with your kids' fathers."

"What?"

"I want to know what happened between you and them."

"Mekel . . . I—"

"Terry, I need to make sense out of all of this." Mekel rubbed his hands across his face.

"I never had luck with men. I guess I had 'easy' written all over my face. It was all good when they got the pussy, but when I told them I was pregnant, they burned out."

"All of 'em?"

"Yup. Then when you came along, you accepted me and my kids. Even after you got it, we were still together. You were different, Mekel."

Mekel's mind played with him.

"I loved you, Mekel. I still do. Truth be told, I could have gotten over you fucking Kera if you were honest about it. But what hurt me the most"—she pointed to her heart—"was the fact that *I* couldn't give you a child. *I* was your woman and I couldn't do that for you."

"You underestimate the ability of a man to overlook the obvious."

"What do you mean by that?" Terry asked.

"What I'm saying is that you are being too hard on yourself. I'm far from perfect, and I didn't have to do what I did."

Terry was silent as she listened.

"And just because you didn't carry my flesh and blood doesn't mean your kids couldn't have been like my own in time."

Mekel looked at Terry and saw the woman he once loved. He knew he couldn't be with her, but he could be there for her.

"Now, you tell me something, Mekel, since we're being open with each other."

"What's that?"

"You've seen me at my best and now you've seen me at my

worst. They made me take off my nails and my weave, Mekel. Can you believe that shit?" They both laughed.

"But seriously though, I've accepted you from day one. I know what we had is over, but can you accept me as I am, right now?"

Mekel looked at Terry in her eyes. "Yes. We have a lot of history and friendships can be forever." He didn't think they could get back to what they were before; however, he would help Terry get back on her feet. "And Terry, for the record, I would have loved to have had a child with you."

After that initial meeting, knowing that a jury would decide Terry's fate was hard for Mekel to fathom. He realized her reaction to his actions landed her where she was, so he was partially to blame.

Terry's attorney fought to get the kidnapping charges dropped and won because Terry didn't actually take the baby out of the hospital. Still, there was the looming charge of aggravated assault. Mekel was due to meet with the attorney later on in the day. He took the chance of contacting her once he learned that his son's condition was not due to Terry's actions.

Mekel also took the necessary steps through the Department of Children and Family Services to protect his child and was now his son's primary caregiver.

He hoped that the courts would let Terry go and grant her some sort of probation. He also asked that her children be returned to her. She was a good mother, and should be given the chance to show the courts that she deserved to be with her children. Terry's attorney seemed to think it would work if he stayed by her side.

Mekel was ready to move on with Terry, his son and her children. He now understood the old adage "You never miss what you have until it's gone." He was also bored with Kera, sexually. In their last few encounters, he had to think about Terry in order to get his nut off. Kera had gotten into what the church said about premarital sex and started being stingy with the pussy. She had done a complete 180 degrees from the Kera he used to know. Mekel already felt he'd been suckered into being a father, but there was no way he was going to be suckered into being a husband, no matter what the Bible said. Turning his attention back to his son, he began to read to him.

Kera left the shop, en route to the hospital. She put in disc two of *The Essential Yolanda Adams*, and turned to track number 2. Kera sang along to "You Changed My Life." Thoughts of Mekel weighed heavily on her mind. She called his cell phone again, and again, but he didn't answer. Before she could flip her phone closed, it rang.

"Hello?" she said, anxiously.

"Hey, girl. It's me."

"Oh, hey, Sasha."

"Well, damn, don't sound so happy to hear from me." They were never really friends, just cordial on account of Red. But, both being burned by her strengthened their bond.

"I'm sorry, girl. I just got a lot of things on my mind. What's up?"

"We're on our way back to town."

"Oh, good!"

"Maybe we can go shopping or something when I get there. Blue got some business to take care of and I don't wanna be stuck in some hotel the whole time I'm there."

"I understand. We can go to dinner or something and if you're still here on Sunday, we can go to church."

"O-kay . . . How's the baby?" Sasha changed the subject.

"He's doing well," Kera lied. Everyone didn't need to know her business.

"Have you heard from Red?" Sasha really didn't care but she needed to be on guard just in case she ran into her while she was in town. She knew she would eventually, but she was hoping for later rather than sooner.

"I haven't seen her since she came into the bank with a bogus check," Kera told her.

"Bogus check?"

"Yeah, she came in, dressed to the nines, trying to cash a one-point-six-million-dollar check."

"Get out!"

"Girl, whoever she got that check from put a stop payment on it. You should have seen her face. It was priceless," Kera admitted with a smug grin on her face, emphasizing the word *priceless*. She pulled up to the hospital. "God don't like ugly." The two giggled like longtime friends. "Hey, I'll talk to you a lil' later. I got a run to make."

"Okay, cool. I'll call you when we get to town."

Dreading what she had to face, Kera trod slowly through the hospital and ended up at her son's room. Outside the door she heard children's music coming from inside. When she walked in, she felt like her prayers had been answered. *Thank you, Jesus*, she said to herself. Mekel was there with their son in his arms.

She smiled at the sight before her eyes. "Hi, Mekel."

He turned toward the voice, then turned back and continued to look out of the window, with lil' Mekel in his arms. "Man, one day we're going to travel. You're going to have the best of everything, just me and you."

Kera's heart dropped. *He's actually thinking about moving on without me. Lord, please don't take my baby and my man.*

It wasn't their son's health problems that had driven a wedge between him and Kera; it was the knowledge that she'd neglected to take care of herself in her first trimester, whether or not he was in her life. After researching fetal development on the Internet in the family resource center of the hospital, he became even more angered because he learned the first trimester is crucial in the development of vital organs and systems.

Mekel had made his bed and now he had to lie in it. He realized that the comfort he felt living with Kera for almost three months was only temporary. She was new to him, and it felt right because she didn't hound him like Terry and his other jump-offs, but he realized that he truly didn't know her. He now knew Terry had been with him, unconditionally, regardless of what he put her through. Kera, on the other hand, became a different person after they began living together. The spontaneous woman who Mekel felt was his equal, on all levels, turned into a churchgoing hypocrite. The expensive art that once graced his walls was now replaced by biblical depictions. Kera had vials of holy water and holy oil in each room of the apartment and she forbid him to play his rap CDs on Sundays. *Sunday is the Lord's day*, she would tell him. *Since you don't go to church, you could at least give Him some respect and glory.*

"I'm glad to see you," Kera said as she walked to stand next to him. She reached out and stroked his arm. Mekel looked at her and twisted his lips. He walked over to the crib, placed his son in it and began to walk out of the door. "Wait, Mekel. Can I talk to you for a minute?"

He stopped and turned around. "You already said enough."

Kera sighed. "Look, just hear me out. I was wrong for blaming you for all of this. We can't let Terry's actions come between us."

Mekel looked at her and shook his head in disgust. "It goes back to Terry, huh?"

"Well, yeah."

"You're blaming Terry, but what about you?"

"What about me?" Kera raised her voice.

"The first three months of your pregnancy. Is there something you need to tell me?"

Kera opened her mouth but no words came out.

Mekel knew by her reaction she was busted. "This didn't have to be, Kera, but you elected not to take care of yourself. Is this payback because I wasn't by your side during the pregnancy?"

Kera said nothing as tears welled up in her eyes. She put her hand over her heart as if it were too full for her to even talk about it without breaking down.

"No matter how you felt about me and my actions, your first priority as a *mother* should have been protecting the baby growing inside of you."

Mekel realized he had to get out of the room before he said or did something he would regret. He began walking toward the door.

"Mekel!" Kera ran up on him and grabbed him by the shoulder. "Baby, forgive me! Please, forgive me," she cried. Kera reached inside of her oversize bag, pulled out her NIV Bible and began thumbing through pages. "First John, chapter one, verse nine says, 'If we confess our sins, He is faithful and just and will forgive us our sins and purify us from all unrighteousness.' Baby, let's pray on this. Let's pray that the Lord will deliver and release us from the grasp of the Devil." Kera quickly reached in her purse and pulled out a vial. She opened it, and began sprinkling the oil around the room, saying, "Father God, please bless this safe haven and everyone in it, for the strength to pull through this crisis." She walked over to the crib and put her finger on the vial and moistened lil' Mekel's forehead. "Bless this child, Father God. He is Your disciple. He's here to serve You."

Mekel couldn't take it any longer. He couldn't stand to be near Kera once he learned of her prenatal neglect. "You really need to stop with your holier-than-thou attitude. If you were so holy you wouldn't have abused your body, oh, I'm sorry, you wouldn't have abused the temple that the Lord gave you." Kera's eyes widened at his condescending tone. "You talking all that stuff about forgiveness. Yeah, I forgave."

Kera's eyes shone with a glimmer of hope.

"I forgave Terry and she's coming home." Before Kera's bottom lip could drop any further than it had, Mekel continued, "Don't worry, I'm a take care of what's mine, but you need to go on with your life and get outta my house." Just as he opened the door to leave, Mekel took one last look at Kera. "Don't think I don't know that you've been coming here when I'm gone. Stay away from my son, Kera," he threatened. "Otherwise, I'll be forced to get a restraining order against you. You can get monitored court-ordered visits when he gets out the hospital."

With that, Mekel sprinted out into the hallway and waited for an elevator. He had to get away from Kera. He didn't know what he might do to her if he had to stay in the room with her a minute longer. He didn't want to leave his son, but he felt it was for the best; plus, he could come back later on. He was also hoping that he didn't speak too soon and somehow jeopardize Terry's impending release.

CHAPTER 22

*A*fter meeting with Terry, Chass knocked at the door of the judge's chambers.

"Come in," the judge called.

"Your Honor, I'd like to discuss the case against Terry Washington." The judge motioned to the seat in front of her desk. Chass presented various forms of paperwork.

"Your Honor, the primary caregiver of the child, the father, Mekel Chambers, has dropped the charges against my client."

"Is there a specific reason?" the judge asked, surprised at this new development. "This was a brutal act against not only a child, but a newborn baby."

"Your Honor, it's a long story." Chass told the judge the story in hopes that she would suggest a lighter sentence. "The father of the child wrote a statement." She handed the judge his letter. "The baby does have medical issues; however, they were not caused by the hands of my client." Chass handed her the statement of the physician who diagnosed the baby.

The judge reviewed the paperwork before her. "Miss Reed, I'd like to meet with your client and the counsel for the plaintiff. At that time, I'll make my decision."

The next day, Terry, Chass, Mekel and his attorney sat before the judge.

"Mr. Chambers," the judge said, "is your child's mother coming?"

"All due respect, Your Honor, my son's medical problems are because of neglect on her part. The Department of Child and Family Services has placed my son solely in my care," Mekel said sternly. "I'm the primary caregiver and I make the decisions pertaining to him."

The judge nodded, then looked over her glasses at the four people before her.

"After reviewing everything, I am suggesting probation and parental counseling for Miss Washington."

Terry looked on with tears of joy in her eyes.

"Furthermore, I recommend anger management counseling to help you handle what life throws at you, Miss Washington. The crime you committed against a newborn is despicable, and only because of Mr. Chambers am I able to offer this to you."

Terry looked at Mekel. He grabbed her hands.

"Mr. Chambers, it's stated here that you want Miss Washington to be released into your custody."

"That's right, Your Honor. Because I am partially to blame, I want to be a part of Terry's recovery process." He looked at Terry. "Although I'm temporarily staying at a hotel, I'm in the process of securing a new home for me, my son, Terry and her children." Mekel didn't want to subject Terry to any more hurt than he had already given her by making her live behind Kera, so this was the best for all of them.

"I'll begin working on the paperwork," the judge said to Terry and Mekel. "Case dismissed."

CHAPTER 23

Q had been in solitude since Zeke's funeral and Red made sure to steer clear of him. She faked her grief in public to show that she took Zeke's death as hard as Q. Even at the funeral, she donned a black veil and cried loudly. The average person would have thought she was grieving heavily, but Red was hiding her true emotions: she didn't care about Zeke and was mainly hiding her guilt. It had been two weeks, and she was tired of acting grief-stricken, but at the same time, she didn't know how to console Q. How could she console someone over a death she had intentionally caused?

"Q, I need to make a run. Will you come by the office later and help me set some stuff up?" Q sat expressionless on the living room love seat as he read over Zeke's obituary for what seemed like the millionth time. "Q . . . Q!"

"What?" he answered, putting the obituary down.

"Nothing." Red shook her head and headed into the bedroom to get dressed. *Can't even have a decent conversation with my man,* she said under her breath. She snatched a pair of jeans off of the wooden hanger in her walk-in closet. *It's been weeks since that nigga died and Q still acting like it was yesterday.*

"Red?"

Red gazed up and saw Q standing in the bedroom's doorway watching her dress. His tone of voice was serious, deadly. Right away her antennae went up. *Q was getting suspicious.*

"Yeah, baby, what's up?" She stood up from the bed and pulled her jeans up. She tried to sound preoccupied, innocent.

"When was the last time you saw Zeke?"

Oh shit, she thought. *I wonder if Zeke ever told Q about that small donation.* She was thinking of the five g's she ganked from him after she fucked him. Red fastened her jeans and began to put on her camisole top. "It's been a long time, Q. You and I were together when I saw him last. Why?"

"I was just wondering why or how he got here."

Red stepped into her stilettos. "I don't know, Q." She turned to the gilded mirror, freshened up her face and threw on a fresh coat of lip gloss. "I was at the office preparing for my open house, remember?" She grabbed some of the material she had been working on and shoved it into her oversize bag. Q nodded.

Red studied him out the corner of her eye. *He has no reason to not believe me,* she reasoned with herself. "All right, baby." She kissed Q on the cheek. "I'll see you later." Red didn't wait for Q to respond. She left in haste.

Driving away from the Garden Lofts at Woodward Place, Red admired the modern architecture of Wayne County and the new construction that seemed to appear overnight. Driving out of her community, she made a left onto Witherell Street. Not long before Red made a right onto Broadway, her heart started racing as she saw a figure that seemed to be coming straight toward her car. The man walked slowly in front of her car, staring at her as he crossed the street. "Damn, he look just like Bacon," Red said, panic-stricken.

Bacon had been on Red's mind over the past few days. Subconsciously, she was concerned—she knew he was out there, but where? Red had contacted Bacon's attorney, who confirmed that he was indeed a free man, then hired a private investigator to help locate him. Red knew how Bacon operated and knew that he wouldn't lie low for too long. However, a couple of weeks ago when she went to the hood to distribute fliers for her open house many people asked about him. Some people thought he was still locked up, which confused her even more. She couldn't explain why people were talking about him but hadn't seen him. She was hoping that he had given up on her, but deep down, something in her gut told her it wasn't the case.

With the red light turning green, Red turned right onto Broadway. She busied herself on her cell with returning business calls. She needed something to keep her mind off of Q, Zeke and now Bacon. Over the past week, she'd been interviewed by several local radio stations and had advertised in local newspapers and on billboards for the open house. Red also went to the areas where ballers were heavy and didn't mind spending a dime. Niggas always tried to hide their dope money in Laundromats, barbershops and car washes, and Red knew that. Commercial properties were lucrative to both her and her clients, and she was there to serve them, as long as they served her.

"In other news, in an update to a case we brought you a month ago, a major drug ring has been uncovered in Boca Raton, Florida. The DEA, along with their drug-sniffing canine companions, has discovered over a million dollars' worth of raw heroin. Approximately two million dollars in cash has been seized, along with several properties. Multiple arrests have been made. We will bring you more news as it becomes available."

Bacon exhaled after the story. He hadn't realized he was holding his breath. *That could have been me,* he surmised and got up to turn the television off. Bacon reflected on how his life had changed.

Black Tar heroin was huge in Mexico; but it was hard to get to the States. Courtesy of Jose, Bacon had brought it in and it had been flowing nonstop ever since. It was now the biggest thing that to hit the streets of Detroit since X. What made Black Tar desirable was the fact it was undetectable by routine drug tests and narcotics-sniffing dogs. Because of this, addicts who were in denial came out of the woodwork looking for a hit.

For the first time in Bacon's life, he called the shots and instructed others to do the dirty work. The women he encountered, unlike Red, felt he was powerful and rich, which boosted his ego, unlike Red, who didn't appreciate anything he did for her.

Bacon had made more money in the three months since he'd been released than the three years he had lived with Red, who spent his dough as fast as he made it on the streets.

Looking back, the one thing he learned dealing with Red was to be on top of his game and not to let a woman run his shit. To pass time, when he wasn't fucking Foxy, Bacon had his share of women, courtesy of Maurice. All colors, shapes and sizes. With pussy almost every night he had his game tight and had gotten back into the drug game with a vengeance. He was untouchable and on top of the world. Bacon felt like he was God because he controlled the destiny of all of the people around him.

With this new product, Black Tar, the possibilities that were now before him were endless. Even the money he had lost to Red was now merely pocket change; but she had violated one of the Ten Commandments, "Thou shall not steal," and she had to be taught a valuable lesson.

Bacon's transformation meant he had no need to travel the grounds he'd already traveled. This time around, he had people working for him to do this. Now he knew how white-collar criminals operated. Now he knew how to stay beneath the law's radar.

After pulling up in front of the prison, Red sighed after seeing how far she had to walk. Thinking about all she had to do, she considered turning back around and leaving. Instead she popped open her glove compartment and pulled out a handicap parking permit that she'd taken from Gloria's desk. Red hung the blue-and-white tag from her rearview mirror and parked her vehicle merely steps from the front gate. It looked like multiple duplexes, surrounded by well-manicured landscape and modern fixtures. The only thing that reminded her of prison was the entry process.

After the mandatory processing, Red was escorted to the visiting areas, where she sat waiting for Catfish to emerge. She looked around the facility and felt dirty. *It's something about this jailhouse air*, she said to herself, looking forward to a thorough cleansing when she got home. She glanced again at the door marked "Prisoners Only" and saw him walk through it.

Oh, shit, look at that greasy bastard slithering over here. Gotdamn, Sasha, you need an Academy Award for even kissing this son of a bitch. Ooh . . . and you fucked his ugly ass, too? I don't care how good the dick was or how deep his bankroll ran . . . shit! Damn, it don't help that his face is wider than a muthafucka.

Red envisioned whiskers growing out of his face, which would make his punch-bowl mouth more prominent. The visual put a smirk on her face. *Gotdamn, boy, you look like a microwaved shit sandwich. Damn!*

While Catfish walked toward Red, his thoughts ran rampant.

I ain't believe the shit when she wrote me, but it's true, she ain't dead. Where the fuck is Sasha? Can't send a bitch to do a man's job. Glad my nigga on it, though . . . two for one. Look at her sitting there, smiling at me with her dirty ass. That nigga Bacon ain't know how to treat her. That kinda bitch needs her ass kicked every now and then to keep her in check. Sasha oughta know. When I find that ho, it's lullabye time, then time to say good night, Red.

"Hi, Catfish!" Red sang cheerfully. She embraced him and kissed his cheek. *Ooh, shit, I'ma need some alcohol.* "You're looking good!"

She sat through an hour visit with Catfish, with her mainly talking about old times and him going along with her game.

"What I really wanted to talk to you about was this." She handed him a copy of *Bitch Nigga, Snitch Nigga.* "The shit in this book can hurt a lot of people."

"Why you bringin' it to me?" he questioned, trying to figure out her motives.

"Because Sasha fucked up when she wrote this."

"Sasha?"

"Yeah, wasn't she with you when all this went down? I'm tryin' to squash shit before it gets started. This has enough information in it to hurt both you and Bacon, especially now that he's out."

"Out?"

"Yeah, he's out." Red planted the seed she needed. She knew that Catfish and Bacon went to prison on the same murder charge. She would get back at Bacon, but she needed help. "You ain't know?"

Catfish remained silent.

"Well, since he's out, I'm sure you'll be out soon, but we need to see what's up with Sasha and why she wrote this shit," Red said, pointing toward the book. "Me and Bacon gon' try to move on and we don't need no shit standing in our way."

Red tried to suppress a smile when Catfish looked at her. His lazy eye refused to focus on her. "I'll get back witcha after I get through readin' this." Catfish got up from the table.

Red watched him stalking toward the door for prisoners. *Ewww, yuck!* she said to herself as she walked out of the room.

Red drove back home to check on Q and to see if he would now consider going to the office with her. She dropped her purse and cell phone on the coffee table, then walked to the bedroom. Q wasn't there. Wondering where he could have gone, Red sat down on the love seat. Realizing where she was, a chill ran up her spine. She was sitting in the exact same place Zeke was sitting when he drank the tainted water.

Red blinked her eyes as visions of Zeke flashed through her mind. *Help me,* she remembered him saying and reaching his hand out toward her.

Her cell phone rang and startled her. Red jumped. "Shit!" She grabbed the device off the coffee table. "Hello?" she said breathlessly.

"Miss Gomez?" the caller on the other line said.

"Yes, who is this?"

"This is Terry Washington's attorney, Chass Reed. I'm calling you because your name has been listed as a character reference."

"Character reference for what?"

"She's being released."

Red paused momentarily, then spoke. "Oh, great!" she exclaimed in fake excitement. *Bitch gonna give me my shit*, she thought.

Red listened to the caller and assured her that she would do what was requested—write a character reference; however, what

Red planned on doing was sending a copy of Terry's taped confession of yet another attempted murder instead.

Red sat back on the couch with a look of satisfaction on her face. "I think this calls for a celebration."

Red quickly showered and the thought of food caused her stomach to growl. She decided to splurge on herself. Andiamo Italia was one of Detroit's upscale Italian restaurants. Red loved the place; however, Q hadn't taken her there in a while.

She knew she had to look on point because it wasn't your run-of-the-mill restaurant. It was one of Detroit's finest and she wanted to look her best. The way the orange Versace fabric of her pantsuit jumper rested against her caramel skin, Red knew she was hot. The Jimmy Choo sandals with matching bag only accentuated her package. Red was fierce and she knew it.

Bacon sat back on the couch, scratching his balls through his boxers, and thought about all he had been told about Red, her business and her upcoming open house. He even learned that Q got out of the game and was spending a little time with another female. Although Bacon was still mad as hell with Red, for some reason, he still wanted her. He just couldn't let her get away with her shit.

Bacon flicked on the television to get his mind off her for a minute, and there was a commercial for Pampers playing.

He thought back to the baby she lost. He remembered she named some people as the cause of her miscarriage. Until now Bacon had forgotten about it. He made a point to ask Foxy about this. Although he couldn't stand Red, someone had killed his seed, and that person would have to pay. But what he didn't know was that she was claiming Q's baby as well.

• • •

Red made it to the restaurant just as a black Cadillac Roadster passed her. It was hard finding a parking spot. She surveyed the parking lot and just so happened to see a car that looked vaguely familiar to her. Red walked into the restaurant as if she had not a care in the world.

"Your name?" the hostess asked.

"Gomez," she responded.

The hostess looked at the reservation list. "Do you have reservations?"

Red glanced down at the list and something caught her attention. *It couldn't be,* she said. *This is my lucky day!*

Soft music played in the background while the decadent scent of baked breads topped with Italian seasoning filled the air. Candle centerpieces at each table provided just enough light for their patrons. Various waiters passed Red, balancing trays filled with plates of meatballs and pasta sauce gracefully on their shoulders. The sight made Red's stomach growl and her mouth water.

"Actually, I was meeting some friends here," Red lied. "We were meeting in the private dining area." Red hoped they wouldn't ask any questions. "I believe they said private dining area two."

"Oh, sure," the hostess said with a smile. "Follow me."

Red followed her to the private dining area but excused herself to the bathroom first.

Red almost had an instant orgasm, thinking of the surprised look that would be on Sasha and Kera's face when she crashed their party.

"Can you believe that bitch had the nerve to call my house, girl?" Kera asked Sasha. "Talking about let me speak to Mekel. Bitch, please!" Kera's religion went out of the window when she spoke about Terry.

"Yeah, she was wrong for calling your crib," Sasha co-signed. "He obviously chose who he wanted to be with, so it's time for her to be a woman and let the shit go. But the fucked-up thing is, she had the nerve to ask about your baby." Sasha took a sip of her water, then shook her head in disgust.

Red had heard enough. Although she agreed that what Terry did was wrong, Sasha's comments angered her even more. She was certain Sasha would pull that card if indeed she was fucking around with Blue. *For her sake, she'd better not be.*

"Ladies!" Red screeched with a fake smile on her face. "Having dinner without me?"

Both women looked on in horror as Red startled them. She sashayed over to Sasha and hugged her, then to Kera and hugged her, as well.

"Y'all look surprised to see me," Red teased.

"What . . . what are you doing here, Red?" Kera asked.

"I should be asking you the same thing. I thought you would have been at the hospital with your child." Red overheard Q having a conversation with Mekel and learned of Kera's son's condition. She sat at to the table, which was set for three, noticed a bottle of Chardonnay in a sterling silver wine chiller on the table and poured herself a glass.

"What's wrong with the baby?" Sasha asked, instinctively.

Kera looked at Red, tightened up her lips and squinted her eyes.

Red turned the Chardonnay bottle and and read: "According to the Surgeon General, 'women should not drink alcoholic beverages during pregnancy because of the risks of birth defects.'" She put the bottle back. "Isn't that right, Kera?"

Sasha watched the nonverbal exchange between the two.

"What's going on?" she eventually asked.

Red then looked at Sasha. "It was fucked up that Kera would mess with her girl's man, isn't it, Sasha? But wait a minute." She sat back, took a sip of wine and continued, "I guess you don't feel that way. What did you say earlier . . . something about being a woman and letting the shit go?"

Sasha glanced away. Red took another sip of the expensive wine, and a figure caught her attention. She almost choked. She couldn't believe her eyes. It was true. Blue came strutting in, looking just as good as he did when she first met him. Not that old wet-goat look he had when he came to town before. Not noticing anyone but Sasha, Blue made a beeline right to her.

"Hey, ma. Sorry I'm late. Business took longer than I thought." He kissed Sasha on the forehead, then looked toward the third place setting and saw Red. "Ooh," he said, " 'sup, Red."

Red responded with a nod while her eyes darted back and forth between the two. *What was going on?*

Blue sat next to Sasha. "I know you ain't drinkin that shit, are you?" He pointed toward the wine bottle.

"No, it's sparkling water." She lifted her glass for him to smell.

"What the fuck you so concerned about, Blue?" Red spat, noticing the closeness between the two.

"She didn't tell y'all yet?" Blue reached toward Sasha's belly and began to rub. "We're having a baby. Your nigga Blue gon' be a daddy!"

"You're pregnant? You got this bitch pregnant?" Red shrieked at Blue.

Kera leaned back in her chair to watch the exchange between the three. She was glad the heat was off of her.

"You self-righteous, pussy-eatin' bitch," Red yelled at Sasha. "You know you ate my pussy because I told this nigga here to make you do it. And yo' dumb ass did!" Red looked at Blue and asked, "How you know that lil' fucker is yours?"

"Yo' game ain't even tight no more. Yeah, I ate your stank-ass pussy, but you know what . . ." Sasha's voice became direct.

"I got your man, and unlike when he was with you, he ain't leavin' me."

Red looked at Sasha, then back at Blue. His expression spoke loudly to Red. "You cum-tastin' heifer, I'ma kill you!"

Blue started to speak in defense of Sasha, but she quickly stopped him.

"I got this." Sasha had to break it down to Red and divulge the real truth. "Bitch, you supposed to be dead. Catfish wanted me to kill you. Only because I'm your friend, you're alive. You got your man. Now let me be with mine!"

Red was momentarily taken aback at Sasha's admission. "You know what, you pissy-ass heifer . . ." Red picked up the wine bottle and threw it across the room. "If that muthafucka wanted me dead, he had the opportunity to do it himself when I visited him the other day instead of trying to have your bitch ass do it!"

Red was incensed because she'd unknowingly put herself in danger when she visited Catfish. The sole purpose of her visit was to feed him information about Bacon and snuff him out of hiding, but now . . . Thinking about all that had transpired, Red stopped going after Sasha, and a sinister smile spread across her face. She now realized that she'd sealed Sasha's fate, with a kiss, six feet under.

Blue's eyes widened. He didn't know that Sasha was Catfish's woman. All he knew was that he was supposed to bring her to Catfish, and now he knew why. He now knew that she was the one they were talking about in the book. She was the one who was a decoy for Q's uncle. What's more, Catfish now knew that Red wasn't dead and Blue would have to answer to him for that. *Oh, shit, what am I gonna do now?*

CHAPTER 24

*R*ed sat outside of Andiamo Italia in the back of a patrol car and watched Sasha and Blue drive away, with Kera following quickly behind them. They were questioned only for a few minutes then let go. Their stories correlated with one another, which pointed the finger straight at Red. The patrol car took off and as Red rode in silence, she briefly thought back to Terry, realizing she had switched places with her. *Scandalous muthafuckas,* she said to herself. *It ain't over!*

When she threw the empty bottle of wine across the private dining area, it unfortunately almost hit their server in the head. That, plus the fact that other patrons were upset at the screaming argument, caused the manager to call the police. This was not a common scene for the crowd who patronized the high-end restaurant.

The young black officer walked Red into the station and escorted her to a small room. He left her there while he ran a fifty on her name. The young officer wanted to know if she had any priors. He came back and sat across from her while information was being gathered. *I've seen her somewhere before*, he said to himself.

"Is there a problem, Officer?" Red asked, feeling uncomfortable with his gaze.

"Nah, nothing. I just gotta make sure you ain't no criminal or nothin'." He laughed.

"Do I look like a criminal?" Red batted her eyes, feigning an innocent look.

"Looks can be deceiving," he said seriously. "Just hold tight."

"Well, I can't go nowhere," she said sarcastically as she held up her handcuffs.

"You know," he said cautiously, "what's a woman like you in there causing a scene for . . . especially over a nigga? From the looks of it, I'm sure you don't have a problem getting any man you want."

"Oh, trust me I don't," Red reassured him snobbishly, "but I ain't gonna be disrespected, either."

The officer shook his head. Someone brought him a report and he perused it. "Other than a small traffic violation, it looks like you're clean."

Red looked at him like, *I know, nigga.*

The officer looked at the report again and it was something familiar about the address. Something he had seen recently.

Damn, that's where I know her from! The officer remembered seeing her picture when he searched Q's apartment for evidence of foul play when Zeke was found.

Officer Thomas put the paper down and looked at her. "So . . . how's Quentin?" Red remained silent. "I was the officer on duty when he called about his friend, Ezekiel."

"Umpf . . ." Red shrugged her shoulders. "Since I'm clean, can you take these handcuffs off of me? You have no reason to hold me here."

"Well, generally I would have to book you on a disturbing the peace charge since you were clownin' in a white restaurant, but since you don't have any priors, I can just issue you a court summons." He started writing in his book and handed Red a yellow slip of paper. "Before you go, can I ask you a few questions?"

"Go 'head . . . hurry up," she snapped.

Officer Thomas got up and walked toward Red. She rubbed her wrists after he unlocked the handcuffs. "How well did you know Ezekiel Morrison?"

"I didn't know him well at all."

"Umm . . ." he grunted. He tried another tactic. "What happened when he came to your apartment?"

"Loft," Red corrected. "We live in a loft, not an apartment."

"I'm sorry, ma'am," he apologized. "What happened when he came to your loft?"

Red's eyes nervously darted around in an attempt to find something to say. "Look, I don't know who murdered him," she said in haste, "but I do know one thing, you're holding me against my free will and—"

"If I recall correctly, I asked if I could ask you a few questions and you complied. I'm not holding you." He held the silver handcuffs up in his hand. "You already have your ticket and you didn't have to answer my questions."

Red looked at the officer with a twisted look on her face. "And if I didn't answer them?"

"Well . . . I would have had to let you go," he said nonchalantly, all the while peering closely at Red. "You can go. Sorry to bother you."

"How am I supposed to get back to my car?" Red asked, remembering she was brought to the station in the back of a patrol car.

"Call someone." Officer Thomas pointed to a pay phone and walked away.

Fifteen minutes later, Northwest Express Cab dropped Red off in the parking lot of the restaurant. She didn't want to call Q because she would have to explain why she was showing her ass. Red walked swiftly toward her car. She wanted to get out of the parking lot and away from what had happened. The cop bringing up Zeke's name had spooked her and she prayed she didn't look uncomfortable in front of him. She was tired of hearing his name. *Let dead dogs lie,* she thought to herself as she drove off and headed to the office. She had one thing to do before going home for the evening. She'd had a full day, and tomorrow promised to be even worse.

Back at the station, Officer Thomas thought about his interaction with Red. *I never said he was murdered.*

Q sat in his car, looking at Zeke's grave through watery eyes. "Man, I got so much to tell you." Q didn't realize just how close he and Zeke were until he was gone.

Q was thankful that he had Chass and her support after Zeke's passing. She became his strength when he needed it. Red just didn't give a damn. Old feelings were beginning to spark and Q just hoped that Chass felt the same way.

Q reflected on the conversation they had over lunch an hour ago.

"Quentin, I don't hate you," she told him after his admission that he thought she did. "I understand a lot more than what you think." Terry had confided in her about her life, which included Red. Chass understood the life of a hustler and, truth be told, if she and Quentin had stayed together, she probably would have left him. She couldn't have been involved with him and his street dealings, considering she was going to law school. "I'm a big girl, Quentin. I'm over it. I'm just glad that we could sit and talk to each other." She gently touched his hands.

Q smiled at her. "You've always been resilient," he admitted. "Your man is lucky to have you."

Chass knew what he was doing and she played into his hand. "Man? I don't have a man. I got so much going on right now, I don't have time for a relationship."

"Well, just know that any man who gets you will be a lucky one." They smiled at each other and continued with their lunch.

Q's thoughts were interrupted when his cell phone rang. Looking at the caller ID, he saw that the number was blocked. "Hello?" he said gruffly.

"Mr. Carter?"

"Who dis?"

"This is Officer Thomas. Could you come down to the station for a minute. I'd like to talk to you about Ezekiel Morrison's death. I received some additional information."

"Sure." Q sighed. "I'll be there." Normally he would have steered clear of the police, but he wanted to find out what happened to his friend.

Twenty minutes later, Q sat across from the officer in his small office.

"Thanks for coming, Mr. Carter." The officer sat back in his black high-backed chair. "Can you tell me again what you know about your friend's death?"

Q immediately started to get upset. He had told his story twice. Once at the loft and once at the hospital. "I've already told you what I know, man. What are you getting at?"

"Raven Gomez."

"What about her?"

"Where was she during this entire ordeal?"

"Why?" Q stood up, defensively.

Officer Thomas looked at Q, then grabbed his pen and started twirling it through his fingers.

Q shook his head at the officer in disgust and began to walk toward the door. Just as he reached the door, the man spoke.

"The cause of his death is still unknown; however, I just spoke with Raven earlier. Why does she think Ezekiel was murdered?"

CHAPTER 25

*M*aria went back and forth between the States and Mexico. She was a mule, the link between Bacon and Jose. Bacon and Maria agreed that their arrangement was strictly business, but after fucking him the night of the cruise, Maria had gotten addicted to the dick. She didn't care if she was a mule; as long as Bacon mounted her like one, it was well worth it.

Foxy was good but Bacon needed a woman's mouth to suck his dick and he craved some pussy to eat. Foxy had begged him to fuck her in her ass, but Bacon was waiting for the right moment. It would come soon enough. He was glad he had another pussy to nut up in, but he kept thinking about Red. Maria was cool, but she had her own money. She couldn't hold down being wifey very well because she was very opinionated and had no loyalty. Red, however, knew her role and played it well, but loyalty wasn't in her vocabulary. She was out for one person, and one person only, the notorious R-E-D.

"Hey, papi," Maria said as she walked through the door of

Bacon's house with two shopping bags from Tappers and one bag of groceries from Hiller's Market. She strutted over to him and pursed her lips. She'd brought some product to town and decided to stay a few extra days.

"You get that taken care of?" he asked as he reciprocated with a kiss. "Didn't have any problems, did you?" He took the Hiller's bag and walked into the kitchen.

Maria walked behind him and watched as he put up the food. "No problems at all. There were no questions asked, and no one really even looked at these." She handed him two small plastic cards and a fat green banking pouch. Bacon loved how she was down for him. Red was never this loyal to him.

She slurped on a strawberry-banana smoothie she bought from the deli at Hiller's and Bacon instantly became aroused. Her head game was right up there, running neck and neck with Red's. Bacon started to miss how Red's pussy felt because it had been a long time since he had been inside her creamy walls, but Maria was a different story. Although she was Jose's connect, she served her purpose well. Bacon didn't want to get too close to her because he knew it would only mean trouble, but this was business, and business had to be taken care of. Fucking was just an added bonus.

Maria saw how Bacon looked at her. She sipped more on her drink and allowed some of it to dribble from her lips onto the cleavage that was exposed by her silk blouse. Bacon walked over to her. "Let me get that for you." He licked the sugary substance off her chest.

"Ooh, papi," Maria moaned, moving his head lower, "you do that so well."

Bacon took her cue and lifted one of her heavy breasts out of its holder and began circling her nipple with his tongue. Maria did her best to unbutton her blouse to give him full access. Bacon loved Maria's breasts. They were firm and more than a mouthful, way more than what Red had.

Maria somehow managed to slip her skirt down and it was now gathered around her ankles. She stepped out of it. Bacon smelled her familiar sweet pea scent and looked up at her. She smiled devilishly as he lifted her up and sat her on the center island of the kitchen. Maria spread her legs to give Bacon a clear view of her pussy.

Hungrily, he buried his head between her legs and began to lap up her juices while she fucked his face. Nearing the brink of an orgasm, Maria became forceful. "Fuck me, fuck me now!" she demanded, pulling his face away from her pussy, grabbing toward his manhood. Bacon's erect penis was already peeking through the opening of his boxers, so it was only a matter of seconds before he dipped into her honeywell.

Bacon enjoyed the way her pussy grabbed his dick like a vacuum. *It must be that Mexican shit,* he thought. He had been in a lot of pussy before but none compared to hers, not even Red's.

Bacon knew that Maria came before he got his nut, and he was pleased with that. She wore herself out attempting to keep up with him, but just as he was about to break off into her, he cupped the bottom of her ass and pulled her toward him. Bacon coated the inside of her vagina with cum and continued thrusting until he was completely drained. Maria wiggled around to make sure she received his last drop. Bacon withdrew himself and watched as their juices flowed from her pussy onto the plastic cards she had given him earlier. He forgot he had it in his hands when he lifted her up on the countertop. Maria looked down in between her legs, then looked up at Bacon.

"That's all you had?" she teased. "I want more." She hopped down off the counter and headed toward the bedroom singing, "Come on, Isadore . . . I have something for you."

Bacon laughed out loud. His eyes zeroed in on the cum-streaked papers that sat before him. "Lisa Lennox," he read, then he looked further. "Gomez Realty." Then he saw another ID with the name Raven Gomez.

Little did Red know, Maria had signed a quitclaim deed to her business in the name of Raven Gomez. *If I can't have shit, neither will she,* Bacon thought. Bacon also had an inside connection at a bank that Foxy had hooked up for him some weeks ago. Maria was allowed to close Red's Gomez Realty account and open one up in Lisa Lennox's name, into which she deposited the advance check that was sent from Triple Crown. Maria also withdrew money from Red's personal account and brought it to Bacon. Maria thought Red would have had more, at least twenty g's more, and according to Bacon, she did, but she didn't argue with the teller. The teller received a handsome payout for allowing the transaction to go through; however, she had been skimming money all along as well.

Maria didn't leave Red completely broke, though. Bacon opened the money pouch that Maria handed him earlier. From the looks of it, Red was on the road to paying back what she had taken from him. Then he looked at the bank slip. It read, "Available balance: $1."

Fair exchange ain't robbery.

At the office, Red sat behind her desk, trying to calm down from what she had just been through. Sasha and Blue, then dealing with the cop. "What could happen next?" she asked herself, exasperated. She looked around the office and admired all she had done. Red had exquisite taste and it was evident. She had spent a lot of money getting the open house together as well as the incidentals of getting a business transferred over into her name. Red was used to having her hands on loot anyplace and anytime she could get it and now she felt like she was poverty-stricken.

Money was not an issue to Bacon, nor was it to Q, until now. *Nigga decide to go legit now,* she said to herself, concerned with the mere fifty g's she had left in her checking account. For a bitch like Red, this meant she was broke, and it wasn't a good feeling.

Frustrated, Red got up and did a final walk-through. "Everything looks good," she said out loud. "I can't believe the open house is going down tomorrow." She walked to the front door and opened it. Dusk was settling upon Detroit, and she looked up at the sky. "Thank you, Gloria. Thank you for all you have done and don't worry . . . I got you, down here."

Red placed her introduction packets on her display table and made sure there were enough home ownership materials and commercial property listings available for her customers. She also placed the latest copies of *Ebony* and *Essence* on the lobby table because they both featured African Americans and home ownership articles.

Red skimmed through the publications to make sure she didn't miss anything before she left for the night, and something caught her eye. It was March's bestseller list. Red read through the section. Her eyes widened when she saw *Bitch Nigga, Snitch Nigga* was number one. "I wonder how much this book has made so far? I only got half upfront, but shit, I know there's money somewhere." Red grinned greedily. "I'm about to get paid!"

"Hi, baby!" Red said, excitedly, when she walked into the loft. It was late and she was glad Q was waiting up for her. She was floating on cloud nine, knowing that she had money coming to her from the book. She kissed Q on the cheek and gave him a tight hug.

"Hey, baby, where you been?" he asked. "I was getting worried about you." He still cared for her but his feelings were torn between Red and Chass.

"Getting ready for tomorrow. You comin', aren't you?"

Q saw Red's enthusiasm and smiled. "Wouldn't miss it for anything in the world." Red kicked off her shoes and plopped down on the couch. "I'm proud of you, baby," Q told her and sat down next to her.

"For what?" Red looked at him. No one had ever told her that before.

"Because you've really made a big change. You're really working hard, Red, and I see it." Red beamed with appreciation. "Oh, I been meaning to ask you, did you deposit the check?"

"What check?" Red was still basking in Q's compliment.

"You know, the check for one point six million."

Red's expression changed almost instantly.

"What, Red?" Q asked suspiciously. "You know I'm outta the game. What was it that you said to me at the church? 'Q, I would trade all of this in for you. I realized it doesn't mean anything if I can't have you.' What are you waiting for, Red? You don't mean it anymore? If not, we can cut our losses and go our separate ways right now." Q was serious. He couldn't allow his pride to be wounded again.

Red's quick thinking took over. "You know what," she said as she climbed onto him and straddled his lap. "I was just thinking . . ." She kissed his neck.

"Thinking about what?" Q said, disgusted.

Red whispered in Q's ear while she unbuttoned his shirt. Q's little head won the battle again. "I was thinking the same thing." Q picked her up and carried her to the bedroom. Red was glad her plan worked; at least sexing Q would buy her some time before she had to tell him about the check.

CHAPTER 26

*R*ed was amazed at the turnout for her open house. The morning was filled with couples looking to buy their first homes and others looking to move into something bigger. She had to endure bratty-ass, unmanageable children who stepped on her new Montablanco shoes, while others ran amok and took the magazines out of the racks and touched the "shiny things." She wondered if, had the parents known their kids would turn out to be brats, they would have elected to take the RU486 abortion pill.

Just as Red expected, the afternoon brought out the ballers, many of whom she had known when she dealt with Bacon. Some thought she was still with him, but others knew she wasn't and tried to get up on her. Red's other real estate plans including flipping houses and hustling HUD deals. Red loved the attention but reminded them that it was business first.

After her last potential client left, Red sat at her desk, exhausted. She began separating the paperwork into requests: inquiries, homes to search for, commercial properties to search for. She also made note of which inquiries would achieve the highest commission. Those would be the ones she would work the hardest for first.

She thought back to a conversation she overheard when she was writing a contract earlier. Although she didn't know who was talking, the message came through loud and clear.

"Man, what you think about that shit I gave you the other week?"

"Had to check it out on the low-low though because I ain't want folks knowin' I was reading like that." Quiet laughter. "Anyway, I wish I could find that ho who wrote the book. I ain't seen her picture on the Triple Crown website, but I wonder if she fine."

"Shit, ain't no need to be fine . . . the bitch is paid. Last thing I heard, she made over a hun'ded g's and the chedda still rollin' in. A nigga need a bitch like that holdin' down some legit shit."

By the time Red finished up with the contract, she couldn't find the culprits who had just called her a bitch and a ho, but her mind was spinning with the information it now contained.

Remembering how much work she had put into everything today, Red knew she would actually have to work twice as hard to live the way she wanted—and this wasn't something she was prepared to do. Looking at the paperwork before her, Red knew through her real estate experience that half of the contracts wouldn't materialize. Either people would change their minds or their credit would be fucked up. She knew the high rollers would want some pussy in return for the fat-ass commission she would receive off their purchase. Her left eyebrow raised at the possibility because some of them were endless money pits.

Do I really want to do this? Do I really wanna work this hard? She stifled a yawn, then thought back to the conversation. Red picked up the phone and dialed. A recording picked up:

"Thank you for calling Triple Crown Publications. Our office is currently closed." She listened to the rest of the message until she heard a beep.

"Hi, this is Ra—Lisa Lennox," Red corrected. "Could you please return my call on Monday morning." She gave her cell phone number and hung up the phone. She straightened up a bit, then left to go home.

Bacon sat outside in his new custom Mercedes Maybach and watched Red walk toward the Range Rover truck she had been driving lately. He had been sitting watching her for the last hour. The more he sat, the angrier he became. "This dirty bitch really came up on account of me," he said, looking at her building, "while I'm sitting in a muthafuckin' cell, wasting away." Bacon could feel the heat from Red's neck in between his hands and feel her esophagus crunch under his power. Like Tupac said in his record, "You can run, but you can't hide."

CHAPTER 27

*I*t was three o'clock in the morning and Blue sat in his car pondering his next move while Sasha slept peacefully in their hotel room. He had just gotten off the phone with one of his street connections and wondered how long it would take before they would act on what he had told them. He and Sasha were due to return to New York later today, but it was also the day Blue would have to report to Catfish.

When Catfish first contacted him about a hit on Red, Blue was down for it. He was still pissed about her fucking up his car years ago when they dated. You can mess with a man, but two things are off limits, his mother and his ride, and Red had crossed the line. However, Catfish didn't know their history and, most of all, he didn't know what Red's pussy felt like.

Blue was checking out the situation when he came to her crib a while back, with the plan to kill her then, but Sasha threw a monkey wrench into the plan. She wanted to fuck, and Blue didn't have a problem with it. What he didn't expect was for the pussy-eating freak to get in contact with him afterward. He knew he wanted to get up in that, because he didn't do it that night, so he didn't kill her right away. However, if Sasha was a dead fuck, he was gonna get rid of her after he got his.

Time was ticking away and Blue would have to report to Catfish not only about why Sasha was alive, but now, Red as well. Blue had a reputation for being a ruthless muthafucka, someone who would deliver, but now his reputation was shot to shit because he didn't deliver. Word on the street had it that death was on the head of the woman who was indirectly identified in *Bitch Nigga, Snitch Nigga*. She was the only one who knew the truth about the murders that night, and Catfish felt Sasha had turned on him, so she had to be silenced. The bounty was quite handsome at $75,000 alive, and $100,000 dead. Greed was a muthafucka. Unfortunately, Sasha knew nothing of the book's contents, but Blue did. He didn't put two and two together until the commotion at the restaurant. Blue looked at the hotel and shook his head.

"Too bad it had to be you," he said out loud. "You were down fo' yo' boy."

He thought back to his unborn child, and without a second thought, Blue started his car and quickly drove away . . . away from all of his issues, and most of all away from Catfish. Once again, Blue was true blue . . . to himself.

Sasha got up a few hours later after a hotel wake-up call. Quietly, she padded around the hotel room. After taking her morning pee, she noticed that Blue wasn't in the room. She peeled back the window curtains. It was a gloomy day outside. The forecast called for clouds and possible rain.

Downstairs, the room service attendant put the finishing touches on breakfast for Room 962.

"Hey, I'll take that for you," another worker offered. "I wanna show Rasheed around the hotel."

"Thanks, guys," the attendant said. "I've pulled a double and I'm tired." She spoke through a yawn.

"No problem." They took the cart and proceeded on the elevator to the ninth floor.

Sasha heard a knock at her hotel door. "Room service."

"Come in," Sasha called out, still peering out of the window. No sooner could she turn around when something that felt like tiny needles pierced her chest, abdomen and neck.

"We got 'er, man."

"Good, we just need 'ta leave tonight to get our money from dat nigga Blue. Bitch niggas, snitch niggas . . ." The other hit man looked at Sasha's dead body. "Just don't need 'em." They left the room.

CHAPTER 28

Red stepped out of the steamy bathroom and Q greeted her with her usual glass of orange juice.

Red didn't have much to say to him because he missed her open house and couldn't give an explanation for his whereabouts. Under normal circumstances, Red would have clowned, but she had other things on her mind. Q slid back into bed. Red noticed it and felt her temper rising.

Another couple of weeks had passed and Q still stayed at home while she worked, but she couldn't let that sway her from what she had to do this morning. She had overslept and was late for an appointment. Red slammed the door hard as she left the bedroom, hoping it would wake Q up permanently for the rest of the day. She jetted out of the front door and rode the elevator downstairs. As she walked to her car, her cell phone rang.

"Hello?"

"Lisa Lennox?"

Red paused for a moment. The name threw her off. Then she smiled.

"Yes, this is Lisa."

"This is Kammi Johnson from Triple Crown Publications. How are you today?"

"I was just okay earlier, but I'm doing well now." She grinned from ear to ear like she was on *Candid Camera*.

"What can I help you with?"

"I was calling about the second payment of my book, and if I have received any royalties."

"Your checks were sent a long time ago," Kammi informed her. "As a matter of fact, I was going to follow up with you again about the sequel to the book."

"Sequel? What sequel?" Red's heart started racing.

"We spoke with your agent, sent correspondence and a contract . . . let's see, almost two months ago about the sequel."

"Agent?" Red questioned. "I had a one-book deal."

"I know but you have had such major success with this book, fans are clamoring for a sequel. As a matter of fact, we would love to have the manuscript by the end of next month. We've already begun working on the cover and—"

"Wait a minute," Red argued. "You're talking like everything is ready to go."

"Well, basically it is, Miss Lennox. We received your signed contract and started rolling on our end. We just need the manuscript."

Red thought for a moment. *Shit, I ain't write the first one. What the fuck am I gonna do now?*

"Ms. Johnson, where did you send the correspondence to?"

"Thirty-one-twenty-four Colonnade Drive."

Red paused for what seemed like forever. "Can I call you back, Ms. Johnson?"

"Uh . . . sure, Lisa," Kammi said with hesitancy. "Just remember, we need the manuscript by the end of next month."

"Can I ask you a question?" Red asked.

"Sure."

"You know, coming up with that first book took some time. What if I am unable to come up with a second book?"

"Well, since the contract has already been signed, it's a legal obligation. If you don't produce the second book, you must repay your advances and any additional fees. Hold on for a minute," Kammi said. Red enjoyed the music while she waited for Kammi to return. "Thanks for holding. As a matter of fact, you should have gotten another check in the mail yesterday, today at the latest. Also, if you cash the check, and don't produce the book, in addition to what I've already stated, you will owe us what was listed in your contract."

"I'm sorry, I don't have the contract with me," Red told her. "How much was it again? I've forgotten the exact dollar amount."

"Fifty thousand dollars," Kammi confirmed. "The advance we sent you was twenty-five thousand."

Red's eyes widened.

"Okay, thanks, Ms. Johnson." Red hung up the phone, completely ignoring what Kammi said about a signed contract. Red had two stops to make when she was done with her client. The first was to the bank and the second was at the house she once shared with Bacon. *I need to get that damn check and his driver's license 'cuz I'm tired of Q bugging me about that damn money. Maybe the advance'll hold him over until I can think of something. Nigga need to find a muthafuckin' job or go back to hustlin'.*

Red's mind flashed to the house and her heart began to race. *I need to get up in my house. If shit's there, then I need to collect.*

But wait a minute, if that nigga Bacon is there, I'd be in danger. Shit, fuck it, I'll just take that chance when I get there.

Q stood in line at the bank with the $1.6 million check in his hands. He didn't understand why Red had never cashed it. He saw it lying on top of their dresser and decided to deposit it into her account. It was already signed, so why not do it for her, he figured.

"Next," the teller called.

Q walked up to the window.

"Hello, Quentin," the woman said.

"Kera? I didn't know you worked here." He didn't recognize her. She wore a long-sleeved shirt, and he noticed she had grown her hair out but wore it in a tight ponytail. Her face was absent of any makeup and Q noticed for the first time how pretty she was. Plain . . . simple. "How are the baby and Mekel?"

A look of sadness washed over her face. "Mekel and I broke up," she told him, "he's back with Terry, they have their own place, but our son is doing well. Mekel is raising him. He's growing and doing better than any of us have expected, all due to the grace of the Lord Almighty."

Q nodded. He remembered Mekel telling him that she went off into this religious kick, but didn't realize how much until now.

"So what can I help you with?" she asked.

Q handed her the check. "I want to deposit this into Red's account. She's already endorsed it, so it shouldn't be a problem."

Kera looked at the check. It was the same one that was no good when Red tried to cash it. "She didn't tell you?" Kera looked at Q quizzically.

"Tell me what?"

"A stop payment was issued on it and I told her that when she tried to cash it." Q hung his head and Kera noticed that his jaw contracted. "Quentin, what's going on?"

"I don't know, Kera, I honestly don't know."

This time Kera wrote VOID on the check and handed it back to Q.

"You trying to say this ain't no good?"

"If Red had anything to do with this, I believe you've just answered your own question."

He walked away, dejected. Being nosy, Kera keyed in Red's name to make sure everything went through in the transaction she had processed a few weeks ago. Kera smiled when she saw that Red's personal account still had one dollar available.

She was being paid handsomely to keep an eye on it. Not long after Red attempted to cash the $1.6 million check, Kera was approached by an attractive woman when she was coming back from her lunch break one afternoon. The woman inquired about opening up an account in the name of Lisa Lennox and Isadore Jeffries. Kera told her that the gentleman had to be present. The woman looked at a well-dressed handsome man. Kera had seen him before but couldn't place where.

"Yo, Kera," he yelled, "lemme holla at you for a second." He learned who she was because people on the street knew her as one of Red's friends.

She looked around and was thankful for customers walking in and out of the bank. She timidly walked toward him.

"Do I know you from somewhere?" She wasn't sure if he was one of the men she fucked before she finally came up, but she was about to find out.

"Depends," he said. "You know Raven Gomez?"

Kera turned and attempted to walk away. She didn't know what she was getting into, but she didn't like the sound of it.

Bacon ran up to her. "Chill, ma, it's all good. You are the Kera who knows her, right?"

"Who wants to know?"

"Did you send this letter to me or did Red send it?" He showed her the letter that he received from Red who was adamant that she didn't send it nor was planning on sending it.

Kera's eyes welled up with tears. "Yes, I sent it," she admitted, realizing that the man who stood before her was Bacon. Kera was scared out of her mind. "Please don't hurt me. Jesus, please send your angels to protect me, I—"

"You need to cut all that yackin', ma. Well"—he scratched his head—"for once in her life, she didn't lie." Bacon looked at Kera. "How would you like to make some money?"

"Su-sure," Kera answered hesitantly. "What do I need to do?"

Bacon gave her one of Red's IDs that she had left at their house. With that in hand, Kera was able to withdraw money from her account from another bank branch. Her own personal payday, she mused. Red would come in the bank high and mighty acting as if she was so much better than Kera. But with every deposit that Red made, Kera took half. Their friendship was like a marriage gone bad. Kera wasn't stupid, though. She had an open account at another bank to deposit the money and would never make very large ones.

She was thrilled that someone else was out to screw Red. *Maybe the Lord will give me some type of reprieve*, she thought. *It wasn't my idea in the first place*. Kera kept a close eye on the Gomez Realty account. When she was through with Red, she wouldn't have a dime. *Lord, please forgive me*, she said under her breath.

• • •

Red walked into the bank around noontime. She'd just finished with her client and before she went to her next destination, she had to check her account. She had tried to check it over the phone, but the phone systems were down. Also, she wanted to throw more barbs Kera's way. Red stood impatiently in line, four people deep.

"Why do they allow tellers to take lunch at noon?" she said under her breath. When it was her turn, she walked regally up to the window. "I need a printout of my available balance," she told the teller. "Your phone systems are down."

"You are aware there is a fee for that, right?" the teller responded.

"Yes. I have more than enough to cover it." Red gave the teller her information.

The computer didn't beep.

"I'm sorry, Ms. Gomez, you don't have enough to cover the printout."

"What do you mean, I don't have enough? Bitch, I got fifty g's in there. Get outta your account, bitch, and get into mine!"

"Ma'am, do I need to call security?"

Red realized she was making a scene. "I'm sorry. A lot of shit has been messed up lately. You were saying?"

"I was saying you only have one dollar in your account."

Red felt like she was about to throw up. "Can you check my business account? It's Gomez Realty."

The teller punched in the requested information. "May I see an ID for that?" the teller asked.

The computer beeped. "I'm sorry, the account has been closed."

"Closed?!" Red screeched. "I wanna see a manager," she snapped. "Y'all doing something shady up here. I know I got money. I cannot be broke!"

The teller called her manager, who came right over.

Red went to the manager's office and explained everything. The manager pulled up a history and displayed it to Red. "Ms. Gomez, on your personal account, it looks like you've withdrawn almost fifty thousand dollars over the last few months."

"That's impossible," Red said.

"I had a feeling you were going to say that, so I've requested the identification that went along with each transaction. Is this you?" He handed her black-and-white copies of her own ID.

Red hung her head. "Yes."

"I'm sorry, Ms. Gomez, there's nothing we can do. You've withdrawn the money from both accounts? I would suggest you budget better next time."

Defeated, Red got up and walked out of the bank. One inside her truck, she broke down in tears.

"No matter how hard I try, legally or illegally, I fuck up. I can't live on the average commission I been making from the agency. I just can't." Red started the truck and began driving toward her next destination. "I know I have money at home, I just have to go get it."

CHAPTER 29

*R*ed drove around the neighborhood in a daze a few times before she parked her car in the familiar driveway of 3124 Colonnade Drive. At her open house, she had re-listed the property as an FSBO, for sale by owner. Attempting to avoid the problem she had before, Red sweetened the deal by offering personal financing and she'd received an inquiry almost instantly. She was due to meet them in twenty minutes. Creative financing to Red meant the buyer would give her a sizable down payment, and she would secure the funding. What the buyer didn't know was that there was no mortgage on the house and every dime given to her, she would pocket. *What the buyer doesn't know won't hurt 'em*, Red reasoned.

Red looked around at the property and winced at the thought of Bacon hitting her with the butt of his gun. She was almost killed in her . . . *Fuck the house and fuck Bacon's ass*, Red said to herself as she sat outside, waiting for her client.

After talking with Kammi, Red was anxious to get inside. She had left some things in the safe and she wanted to get them. Having to show the house was the perfect opportunity. Red saw there was something out of the ordinary about the house. It was meticulously kept, better than what she remembered.

After finding her extra set of keys, she stealthily stepped out of her car and cautiously walked toward the front door. Pausing after her third step, Red looked around. *Something doesn't feel right.* Her legs felt like lead with each step she took. Once she arrived at the front steps, goose bumps rose on her arms and the hairs on the back of her neck stood straight up. The first thing Red noticed was the abundance of mail that was stuffed in the mailbox. Bundling it up, she stuffed it under her arm.

"There you are!" a high-pitched voice screeched.

Red jumped and turned. A feeble older woman tottered toward her from next door.

"Where have you been, young lady? You oughta let your neighbors know when you're gone for an extended period of time," she scolded Red like a schoolkid.

Red smiled sheepishly at the woman. "I'm sorry, Ms. Taylor. I had an emergency out of town," Red lied.

"I hope everything is okay," the woman spoke. "I tried to catch your gentleman friend but—"

"Gentleman friend?" Red quizzed.

"Yes, the extremely tall, slender and might I add, handsome"—the woman patted Red on her forearm to note her approval—"young man I saw coming in and out of here for a few months. He seemed to forget about the mail, so I started collecting it for you. I been a little under the weather lately, so I couldn't get the stuff that's in there now."

A car drove down the street and Red held her breath until it passed. *Why am I so paranoid?* she said to herself. *This is still my house.* Red had to get the old woman away from her. She was wasting her time. "I appreciate it, Ms. Taylor. What can I help you with? I really gotta go . . ." Red shifted from foot to foot, doing an "I gotta pee" dance.

"Oh, nothing. I just wanted to give you this." She handed Red a box. "I collected your mail while you were gone. Didn't want it to seem like nobody was there, you know. There was some type of shooting some time back in the neighborhood. Cops never found out what happened, but you know we have to keep this block safe."

"You're right, Ms. Taylor. Thank you and I appreciate it."

A pleased look of neighborly satisfaction on her face, Mrs. Taylor hobbled away.

As soon as she was out of sight, Red put her key into the lock and prayed it still turned.

Click!

Red stepped inside.

Moments earlier, Bacon eased the curtains back slightly as he peered out of the window. His eyes narrowed when he saw Red park her car in his driveway. Anger radiated from his pores when he saw her emerge from the vehicle. How could he be so lucky? He wanted to jump through the window and strangle her, but he had to play it smart. He would just wait until she came into his web. *It's playtime, bitch . . . and this time, you lose.*

Q left the bank in haste while he angrily punched Red's cell phone digits on his keypad. Before pressing Talk, he snapped the phone closed. "Fuck that bitch and all she stands for!" he yelled out loud. Pedestrians gazed at Q in shock. "Fuck you lookin' at?" he yelled at an old woman who held her purse tightly in her grip when he passed her. He leaped into his truck and skidded off.

Arriving at the loft, Q parked and took the elevator upstairs. His mind was overcome with confusion because he didn't know why Red never told him that the check was no good.

Was she trying to play me at the church? he questioned. *I thought she'd changed.* Q wasn't just upset that the check was no good; it was the fact that Red never came clean with him about it and if she would hold something that small from him, what else would she keep from him? *Every time I trust her, I'm the one who winds up getting fucked in the ass.*

Q went into their bedroom and started taking her clothes out of her closet. Ten minutes later, a large pile was lying across their bed but he hadn't even made a dent in what she owned. His first idea was to throw everything in the incinerator, but then he had second thoughts. He looked through some of the clothes. A lot still had tags on them. He took them to the bathtub and threw them in there. Q made his way to the kitchen and took out a bottle of Clorox bleach. He marched back to the bathroom and emptied the entire bottle of bleach on Red's clothes.

Angrily, he left the loft and made his way back to the bank.

"Hey you!" the bank security guard yelled at Q when he barged past him. "Where you goin' so fast?" The guard put his hand on Q's shoulder.

Q didn't realize how crazed he appeared, or how his behavior could have been looked at as irrational. "Get yo' hands off me." Q spoke through gritted teeth.

"Hello, Quentin," a soft female voice said in a meek tone.

Q turned and looked at Kera.

"Is everything okay here?" the guard asked.

"Yes, everything is fine." She led Q to a sitting area, being careful not to trip over her ankle-length black skirt.

"Quentin, I'm sorry about the check incident earlier," Kera said. "I thought Red would have told you about the stop payment." Q cut his eyes at Kera then looked away. "Listen to me, Quentin, there's more you need to know."

Q sat still and listened while Kera spoke.

"She barged in on me, Sasha and her boyfriend, Blue, at Andiamo Italia some time back and caused a scene. Last we saw of her that night, she was in the back of a patrol car."

"Who is Blue?"

"Some guy she used to mess with a long time ago, but Sasha's with him now. They announced that they were going to have a baby, and Red got upset about it."

"Come on, ma, I don't believe that."

"It's true, Quentin."

Q turned his head and looked out toward the customers who were filing in to make deposits or withdraw money.

"Well, if you don't believe that, then what if I told you she wasn't pregnant the first time she said she was."

"What?"

"I said, the first time Red told you she was pregnant, at the Renaissance Hotel, she wasn't." Kera remembered Red telling everyone she was pregnant by Carlos, who was in a wheelchair, but Kera knew what really happened.

Q thought back to it. He had never told anyone about it, especially the location, with the exception of Zeke, so he knew she had to know something. "The test was positive, Kera. I saw it with my own eyes. It turned pink."

"I know it did." Kera put her head down in shame. "It was my pee."

"What . . . how?" Kera started to speak, but Q held up his hand, cutting her off. "I don't wanna know."

"It's an old trick, Quentin. Anyway, back to the restaurant. I thought things were going well for you all. That's what she led me to believe when she came into the bank before."

At that moment, Q began to question Red's reason for being with him. *Why would she act that way over another nigga when I'm here? I saved her ass from getting killed, but she's pissed that another nigga got someone else pregnant?*

The harsh reality sank in that Red now spent more time away from home because she couldn't handle the fact that Q was serious about getting out of the game. Q was on the legitimate hunt for legal employment but knew it would be a long and tedious road. He only knew how to hustle, had no employable skills that matched the paper he'd been getting. He was hoping that Red would stick by him in the same way he was there for her, but he was mistaken.

Red claimed her absence was due to her new real estate business, but Foxy had told him that word on the street had it that some of the major players planned to go after her. Buy property, get pussy: the bigger the commission the more pussy you got, was the big buzz. Q knew that it was street gossip, but the idea that his woman was so scandalous that her name was on everyone's lips was just too much to handle—especially after Zeke's death. Q was tired of being humiliated.

"Kera." Q looked at her with pain in his eyes. "I want to apologize for Red's actions toward you. But I will say, you messed up when you sent that letter to Bacon. It almost got her killed. Shit, it almost got *me* killed."

"I'm sorry, Quentin. If I could take everything back, I would," Kera answered honestly. She looked at the long line beginning to form. "I'm sorry, but I have to go back to work."

Q nodded and left.

Red slowly stepped into the foyer and looked around, cautiously. She couldn't believe her eyes. The living room was adorned with expensive contemporary furniture and black art. She walked into the kitchen; it was now decorated in a contemporary style, with all stainless-steel appliances and a Sub-Zero refrigerator.

As she walked back from the kitchen to the living room, a cold chill ran through her spine as she realized she was now in the place where she encountered Bacon the last time.

Bacon . . . Bacon, she thought. *Could he be here? Nah,* she convinced herself. She remembered the call she received from the private investigator. She just hadn't had time to return their calls. *Maybe I should have,* she thought as she continued to walk. *If he was out, I'm sure he would have crossed my path,* she reasoned to herself. Maybe he took my advice, turned homo and died. Red grinned at the thought of him getting fucked from behind the same way he did her.

A million thoughts ran through Red's head, then she realized she was still carrying the box that Ms. Taylor had given her as well as the other mail she had retrieved just moments ago. *Maurice Clarence,* she read. The rest was junk mail addressed to her.

"That's the basketball player," she remembered. "That's the person Ms. Taylor must have been referring to. Shit, muthafucka been living in my crib, he gotta pay me some rent, but first things first."

That's right, get yo'self together, bitch. Just get yo' shit and vamp!

She looked at her watch. Her client was twenty minutes late and she wasn't going to wait around any longer. She hyped herself up as she made her way upstairs to retrieve what she felt was rightfully hers. She paused outside the door of the master bedroom. Slowly, Red walked inside and her eyes darted from wall to wall. There was a blue banking bag on the bed, but she quickly walked over to the picture that hung next to the window and removed it. She smiled when she saw the safe. Twenty-four, thirty-six, twelve . . . she turned the combination, hoping it hadn't been changed. She sighed when it clicked, allowing her access.

Red's eyebrows raised when she saw the only thing in the safe was a mirror. "What the fuck is this?" Two eyes appeared reflected behind her. The full face came into view and Red's mouth opened wide at the same time a strong arm grabbed her around her neck. Before she could say his name, she was thrown across the room. Red tried to struggle to her feet. Before she knew it, Bacon pounced over to her and grabbed her by her hair, holding her head back. "You make one fuckin' move and I swear, I'll snap your muthafuckin' neck, bitch."

CHAPTER 30

Q drove away from the bank not knowing what to do. He hated the ground Red walked on and wished that Bacon would have killed her when he had the chance. He looked down at his cell phone and saw that he had a missed call. The ID displayed the Officer Thomas's number.

"What the fuck he want?" Q said out loud. He had been calling him for the past couple of days, but Q never returned his call. He drove to the closest liquor store to find something strong that would wash out the bad taste Red left in his mouth. Q bought a fifth of Martel and hightailed it back to the loft. He wanted to be there when Red came home for the evening so that he could kick her ass out of his house and his life, permanently.

The ringing phone seemed ten times louder to Q. He looked down and saw the empty bottle of Martel. "Stop it," he slurred, reaching over to answer the phone. "Yella."

"Mr. Carter?"

"Who wans ta know?" Q's tongue felt thick.

"This is Officer Thomas. I need to see you about Ezekiel's murder. I just got ahold of the toxicology report and there's something I think you'd be interested to know."

"Yeah . . . yeah . . ."

"I also think you need to know we found a vid—"

Q hung up on the officer. He was tired of the officer's badgering and accusations.

Bacon yanked Red's neck back until he couldn't go any further. He wanted to snap her neck so bad that his dick started to get hard. "Bacon, please," Red cried quietly and a tear rolled down her cheek.

Bacon looked at her, cackled evilly and stood up.

Smack!

He backslapped her.

Smack!

He slapped her again.

Red began to get angry. Not only had he slapped her once, he slapped her twice. She rose to her feet.

"Bitch, I ain't say you can get up." Bacon slapped her again. "You move when I tell you to move." Red got back on the floor. "You dirty bitch!" She had never seen this side of Bacon before. "Now, crawl."

Red wiped her face with the back of her hand, wiping away the tears that were streaming down her face. "B-B-Bacon, you been watchin' too much TV." She remembered how he liked this particular scene in the movie *Sparkle*, but she couldn't play it out for him.

"That's all I had time to do when I was locked down, and you was spending all my shit, so bitch, I said crawl!" Bacon pointed his .357 Magnum toward her. "Or die."

Red knew she should have taken his guns out of the safe when she first thought about it, but now it was too late.

Bacon pulled the blue bag off of the bed and opened it. Red stayed in the position she was in. Bacon reached in and grabbed a stack of money and threw it down by his feet. He reached in and threw another one down. Red knew the band colors that held the money, and he had just dropped 50 g's right in front of her.

"You know you want this. Now you know what it's like to be broke, huh? Crawl!"

Red began crawling.

Bacon reached in and dropped more stacks.

Red crawled more. *Your available balance is $1. Now you know what it's like to be broke, huh?* rang repeatedly in her head. She stopped when she reached his feet. Bacon reached in his back pocket and pulled out a piece of paper. He looked at Red. "What was that bullshit you said to me before?"

"What?" she questioned.

He read out loud in a stentorian voice:

Dear Bacon,

Or, in your case, should I call you John? This is the letter you been beggin' for.

Well, let's see. It would be virtually impossible for you to kick my ass, seeing as how you will be an old and gray bastard when you come home. Your dick is so little that I can't believe you even wear a size 12 shoe. There goes that myth. When I first met you I sized you up real good and I knew the dick was going to be swinging. Boy, was I wrong. I guess that teaches me not to judge a book by its cover, or a dick by its shoe size.

I hope with all the free time on your hands you now realize that I never loved you. As quiet as it was kept, I didn't even like you. Before you got locked up I couldn't even stand the sight of your face, and let's not discuss the sound of your voice.

"Bacon, I told you I—"

He skipped down to the next paragraph and read, "'Your partner Stan's cum tastes like ice cream in my mouth.'" He skipped more. "'I got your loot, you took the case, now press that bunk and do that muthafuckin' time.'"

Bacon's hand began to crumble the paper as he read, "'*My new man and I reap all the benefits . . . get you a boyfriend, let him suck your dick and leave me the fuck alone.*'"

Bacon undid his pants and allowed them to fall on the floor.

"Stan's cum tastes like ice cream, huh?" He grabbed her head and forced it into his crotch. "Suck my dick, you dirty bitch."

Red instinctively moved her face away and Bacon knew why. He knew when he placed the call about wanting to see the property a few days ago, Red would jump at the chance to show it. And she did. Because of this, he made sure that he didn't wash his dick after fucking Foxy in her ass about an hour ago.

"Open up," he sang as he waved his flaccid member in front of her. "Bite me and you're dead." He caressed her face with his .357 and kept the barrel of the gun right at her temple.

What the fuck am I doing? Red said to herself. *Got this nigga's nasty-ass dick in my mouth. I need to get outta here. He's gonna kill me. Lord, please help me.*

Red began to suck Bacon's dick. The more she sucked the softer it seemed to become. Bacon began grinding his groin into her mouth as he let go of a warm liquid. "Yeah, drink it up bitch," he said as he peed in Red's mouth.

Red snatched her head back, but he quickly grabbed his dick and finished the flow trickling on her face.

"You grimy bastard!" Red shouted.

"What it taste like?" Bacon grinned at her. "It taste better than Stan?"

Bacon loved forcing Red into submission. He wanted her to suck his dick again but he had other business to take care of.

"Get the fuck up," he yelled at her.

Red slowly stood up and he motioned for her to get on the bed. "Bacon, I don't—"

"I don't wanna fuck yo' piss-drankin' ass. I wanna play a little game with you, now sit down." He patted the bed next to him.

Hesitantly, Red sat down.

"You heard of the game Russian roulette, right?"

Red nodded.

"Well, I got one bullet in here." He waved his .357 in front of her, "and you have some choices to make."

Red looked at him and rolled her eyes. Bacon grabbed her hair and jerked her head backward. "This game is called Life or Death."

Red peered at him through tear-soaked eyes.

"Ma, look, I still love you."

"You sure got a fucked-up way of showing it!" Red spat.

Bacon's hand tightened on her hair.

"Word on the streets had it you were asking about me."

"Asking about you? Huh . . . I don't think so."

Bacon shook his head. "You really think I'm still that same stupid Bacon you knew before he got locked up, huh? You stole from me when I gave you whatever you wanted. You disrespected my house and let another nigga come over here. I should just . . ." Bacon reached toward her throat and wanted to choke the life outta her, but he stopped.

"I can't blame you, Red, for doing what you did. I mean, I was gone for a while, but you was wifey. I never thought you would fuck me the way you did. But baby, I'm back," he said smoothly. "I got more than you could ever want."

"I don't want you, Bacon!"

Instantly, Bacon let Red's hair go. He gently turned her face toward him. "I can give you the world, Red. Anything you want . . . it's yours."

"I have my own," she retorted.

"No, you don't and you know it, Red. Just for the record, I know everything. I even know about the baby that you claimed was mine. You didn't know whose it was, Red. How you gon' let that pretty-ass nigga nut all up in yo' pussy, then have me go behind him?"

"I ain't make you do shit, Bacon. I ain't wanna fuck you," Red admitted.

"But you did fuck me. The fucked-up thing is, Red, you wanted me to kill someone who killed our baby." Bacon laughed. "Our baby. I can't claim what I don't know is mine, so I ain't fuckin' with nobody over it. Who knows whose baby it was?" Bacon continued talking. "You stole from me. You know what, though? I took back everything you took from me. The money from Triple Crown, your bank account is empty, and the little business you own . . . it's not in your name."

"What you mean, not in my name?"

"You don't remember signing the quitclaim deed?" He shoved the papers in Red's face. "Same shit you did to me, Red, I did it to you."

Red thought about what he had just told her. Her fists began flying. "How the fuck you gon' take my money out of my fuckin' account . . . take my business . . . you dirty bastard!"

Bacon blocked her blows.

"Now you know what the shit feels like. I had to start from rock bottom all because of you. Now, do you wanna know how you can redeem yourself? This will wipe out your debt and we'll be equal. The prize comes with unlimited money, but it requires loyalty. Loyalty or death, Red, which one do you choose?"

"Fuck you, Bacon! I hope you die, you dirty bastard!"

"A nine-to-five ain't you, Red." Bacon ignored what she had just said. "You were made to be wifey. We can go anywhere and get started all over, baby. Just me and you. So . . . what's it going to be? Death"—Bacon cocked the gun—"or loyalty?"

Red paused. She realized Bacon was serious. She gulped a deep swallow of spit before she spoke up in a whisper. "Loyalty."

Officer Thomas got into his patrol car and decided to go to Q's. He had information for him that he thought would be helpful, plus he had a search warrant for the loft. The security camera videotaped the comings and goings that night Zeke was killed. He saw Q enter the building, then an older woman, whom Q left with. Not long after the older woman was seen on video, Red appeared. Officer Thomas noticed that Q and the woman left, but then he saw Zeke enter the building as well. According to the tape, approximately 20 minutes passed before Red walked swiftly toward the exit. Q arrived, then shortly afterward, the police and the ambulance. Officer Thomas knew Red was hiding something when she slipped up and mentioned murder in connection with Zeke's death.

For a man as young as Zeke, without any known medical problems, to die was very suspicious. Now he had proof. Red knew something, but he wasn't prepared for what he had learned.

Red and Bacon arrived at the loft within a half hour. With tears in her eyes, she looked at Bacon.

"Loyalty, remember?" he said to her. "And everything you could possibly want will be yours. I still love you, Red, and on the real, do what I ask and we can charge it to the game, not your heart, feel me? Now come on, let's do the damn thing."

Slowly, Red emerged from the car and walked into the building toward the elevators. Bacon followed behind her. He had to make sure she didn't turn on him. Even though she chose loyalty over death, he wasn't stupid. Red was still a dirty bitch.

Red ignored the doorman's greeting as she looked at the two elevator cars in front of her. They both seemed to take their own sweet time returning to the main floor. Red stepped on the first one and turned around as the door closed. Bacon slid in right before it closed.

Loyalty, Red thought. *Q has done so much for me and I can't forget that. He risked his life for me. If that ain't loyal, I can't say what is, but Bacon . . . he can give me the life I want.* She looked at Bacon, who was staring at her intensely. The elevator continued to climb, now almost at its destination. *Q loves me unconditionally.*

The ding alerted Red she finally reached her floor. She stepped off the elevator with Bacon behind her.

Walking slowly toward the door of her home, Red decided to do something out of the ordinary. *Maybe Q would pick up that something is wrong*, Red hoped. She knocked on her front door and rang the bell. Within minutes, Q opened it.

Red walked in. "Damn, what you been doin' up in here?" she asked. It smelled like a distillery.

"You . . . I can't believe you would do all of the shit you've done to me, Red," Q slurred, talking with no obvious purpose.

"What you talking about?"

"The pee test you did, I know all about that. I know how you played Kera and your girl Sasha. You still dirty, Red."

"Q, you're drunk." Red tried to escort him to the couch. "You need to lay down."

"I don't need to do shit but tell you to leave." He looked closely at her. "Get the fuck outta my house."

"What?"

"You heard what I said, get the fuck OUT!" He pointed toward the door.

"Look, you're obviously angry for some reason. I'm gonna get some clothes and stay at a friend's for a few days."

"Friend? You ain't got no friends, Red." Q then mumbled something under his breath that Red couldn't understand.

She marched to the bedroom but came back in less than a minute.

"Q, where's my shit?"

"Get out, Red."

"Where's my shit?!"

Red realized the pungent smell wasn't Q and his drunken state. It was bleach. She ran to the bathroom.

"You bitch-ass muthafucka! How yo' broke ass gonna fuck my shit up?"

"Easy. I'm just doing what you told me to do in Mexico. You told me to keep the clothes, that they were too much of a reminder of me, so yo' shit was too much of a reminder of you, so I had to do something with them. Fair enough, isn't it?" Q smirked.

"You broke-ass bastard!"

"Broke? That's the second time you called me that and it will be your last. See, that's your muthafuckin' problem. I told you I was getting off the damn streets. I grew up, Red. I was trying to come clean so I could build a better life for both of us, but, naw, you ain't want that. You still on that kiddie shit. You know what? Get the fuck outta my house and my life, Red. Play your childish games for someone who cares."

Q turned around. Red reached into her oversize Marc Jacobs bag and pulled out the gun that Bacon had given her. *Q loves me unconditionally,* she repeated, *but would he die for me?*

"Do you love me, Q?" Red called out through tears. He didn't answer her. "Do you love me, Q?" she asked again.

"I can't love anyone who is as heartless as you."

"*I* love you, baby. Do it," a voice urged.

Q turned around at the sound of the voice. He saw that it was Bacon. "What the fuck?" As drunk as Q was, he charged at Bacon. The two men began to tussle, knocking over furniture.

Without warning, a loud sound rang out.

Pow!

Bacon pulled away from Q and Red watched as Q's body slumped to the floor. Just as she quickly turned to leave the loft, she turned back and looked at Q. Tears ran down her face as she watched him struggle to breathe. No matter how she truly felt about Q, her back was up against a wall and she had to make a decision. Her life or Q's. *She chose to live.*

Acknowledgments

My Lord and Savior Jesus Christ. For this I know that Thou art with me, for He has not allowed my enemies to triumph over me. To my family: the Stringers, the Berrys, the Ranges, the Haggens, the Thompsons, and the Rockefellers.

My sister, Linda Stringer, and my twin—it is such a pleasure to be your family.

Mia McPherson, my right hand and faithfully devoted angel-sent friend.

April Tang, my personal assistant. Thank you for being so superbly wonderful and perfect in all that you do.

My favorite niece, Ruqiayah Stringer. I'm so very proud of you.

To my mother, Eula Thompson and my father, Thomas Range: am I a chip off you old blocks or what? Proud of me?

To my devoted Triple Crown staff and all those devoted, true-blue, rain, snow, sleet and hail fans.

To my editors: Malaika Adero, Krishan Trotman, Donna M. Rivera.

To my writing coaches, Reagen Gomez, Cynthia Parker and Maxine Thompson, thanks for helping VS.

I can't list everyone, but I'm so good at saying thank you I will say it again: Thank you for supporting me.

To my life reasons: Valen Mychal and Victor Amon and Vegas. I love you guys with all of my heart.

Always,
VS